Other books by Scott Ely:

Pit Bull

Starlight

Pulpwood

The Angel of the Garden

Overgrown with Love

Eating Mississippi

by

Scott Ely

Livingston Press
at
University of West Alabama

Library of Congress Control Number 2005928094

Printed on acid-free paper.

Printed in the United States of America,
Publishers Graphics
Hardcover binding by: Heckman Bindery
Typesetting and page layout: David E. Smith
Proofreading: Jennifer Brown, Margaret Walburn,
Tricia Taylor, Megan Edmonds, Larry Cowan, Moneek Bryant
Cover design and layout: Jennifer Brown
Cover art: "Alligator Snapping Turtle, Macroclemys temminki"
Hand-colored etching by William B. Montgomery, Copyright 1994
For more information contact W.B. Montgomery,
P.O. Box 656, Elgin, TX 78621
512-281-0046
montgomery6@earthlink.net

This is a work of fiction.
You surely know the rest: any resemblance
to persons living or dead is coincidental.

Livingston Press is part of The University of West Alabama,
and thereby has non-profit status.
Donations are tax-deductible:
brothers and sisters, we need 'em.

first edition
6 5 4 3 3 2 1

Eating Mississippi

by

Scott Ely

for Susan

Chapter One

ROBERT DAY STOOD in a cloud of dust and surveyed the empty attic. The dust smelled of cypress. Stands of cypress grew along the Pearl River whose banks bordered his front yard. He imagined their feathery tops, their branchless trunks rising smoothly out of the dark water, the polished knees ranged in circles about the parent trees.

All morning he had carried pieces of broken furniture downstairs; he had opened trunks and boxes, throwing most of what he found into a dumpster. His most valuable discoveries had been a silver fork and three crystal wine glasses.

On leave from his job as a translator, he had recently taken up residence in the house on the Pearl River in Mississippi. Two years ago he had lost his wife Elaine, killed by poachers in Africa. An anthropologist who specialized in the study of chimpanzees, she had gone to Africa to continue her research. One day she did not return from the forest. She had been executed, a single shot in the head. So far the police had not found the people who killed her.

After the funeral, after he had made the difficult trip to Africa to bring her body back, he found Elaine's presence inescapable. It weighed him down. It was as if he and their house—a house they had built in the Midwestern town where the university was located—were being slowly ground under by a glacier sliding down from the pole and across the plains. He recalled how a month or so

1

after he learned of her death he found himself reading the draft of a paper Elaine had been working on about aggression in chimpanzees. It was based on her research of several years before. He read only a few paragraphs, wondering as he read why he was reading. Did he think he would find in her paper some sort of explanation for why she was killed? Then he drifted off into a reverie of her walking through the rainforest-covered mountains. He had never been able to imagine her lying dead in the forest. He could see her hand, a foot, or a bit of her red hair, but never any blood. The only thing he could always clearly see was the riot of green, the rainforest, like a giant hand pushed up against a camera lens.

He had tried to lose himself in his teaching and stopped drinking completely. But then one night he found himself sitting at the kitchen table with a .44 revolver in his hand and Mozart playing on the radio. He had bought the revolver as protection against brown bears when he and Elaine had gone fishing in Alaska. He did not think he was particularly depressed, but he felt the urge to put the gun to his head and pull the trigger. Earlier that day he had called up an anatomical chart on the web to determine the best place to send a bullet into his brain. It was the careful rational manner in which he approached the act that frightened him the most. He savored the feel of the cold end of the barrel against his temple, but he never cocked the revolver. He got up, made himself the first drink he had had in months and put the revolver back in the drawer of the table beside his bed.

After that he began to have recurrent dreams of hunting down and executing the men who had killed Elaine. The tracker who worked for the police determined that there were three of them. He told the police how much they weighed. At a river crossing he found the scat of the biggest man. But when the men boarded a truck at the foot of the mountain, the tracker lost the trail. Robert imagined the scat lying frozen in some police lab, awaiting the day when the DNA it contained might prove useful. Robert's dreams took on aspects of scenes from movies. They were larger than life, exceptionally vivid in color and scale. In this dark place in his mind, he painted the green forest with the blood of the poachers. He had never killed anyone; he had never seen anyone killed. Asthma had kept him out of the Vietnam War. The boys he grew up with had gone there and killed people and had been killed themselves and maimed in body and mind.

Now that he had come to live in the house in Mississippi, he found he no longer had those dreams or fantasies of revenge. He lost interest in the infrequent reports from the police that were relayed to him through the American embassy. Africa was a continent filled with death. He had only lost his wife. Others had lost every member of their families from disease or genocide. Gradually he managed to put the pain of losing Elaine in some secret place in his heart. He spent no time with therapists; he refused to talk about Elaine with his friends at the university.

Although he had installed an internet connection so he could access libraries, he corresponded with no one. He had made no friends except his doubles partners for tennis, and he never saw them except when they came out to the house to play or when one of them was playing with him in a tournament.

He had inherited the house and a few acres of land from his aunt, just before Elaine had gone off on her trip to Africa. His family had never owned the house. This aunt was a real estate broker. She had planned to turn the house into a bed and breakfast. But instead of repairing the roof as her first project, she had installed a tennis court. He liked that about his aunt. For some reason he had held onto it instead of selling. Also, no one seemed interested in buying. To restore the house to its former splendor was going to take time and money.

Even though he planned to do some work on the house, he wanted to spend most of his time translating a series of letters written by a French troubadour, not to a lady but to his fellow poets. The letters were written in Occitan. But so far he had rendered only one sentence into English. He translated that sentence over and over, always dissatisfied with the result. Finally he put the project aside, intending to wait until he was ready. He was not sure how he would know that. So he distracted himself. He repaired the ancient plumbing, weeded the overgrown rose garden, and replaced the rotted back porch.

He had spent the last hour sweeping the attic clean, raising great clouds of ancient dust. Already, despite the open windows, it was uncomfortably hot. The birds had ceased to sing their morning songs. The dust, which tasted sweet, fell on him like a gentle rain and coated his sweat-covered bare chest.

The rough, hand-planed cypress flooring, pegged to the joists below, was disturbingly vacant. Only now did he understand that he preferred it cluttered and unexamined. He should have savored the exploration, discovering the attic's secrets slowly.

He walked from one end of the attic to the other, the boards creaking beneath his bare feet, as he examined the floor for signs of dry rot or water damage. In a corner, one of the pegged boards was loose. As he knelt to examine it, he discovered that the short length of board was held by only one peg. He inserted his knife blade into the crack and pried up the free end. He worked the single peg loose; he lifted the board.

In the hollow space was a hinged ivory box whose top had been carved with an elaborate hunting scene, dogs chasing a deer with riders in pursuit. As he picked up the box, he felt something shift inside. He hefted it, delaying the pleasure of discovery.

But when he unfastened the brass clasp, now green with age, the box would not open. It had been sealed with wax. He ran the knife blade along the seam. Then he set the box on the floor. Still he delayed. He sat cross-legged, holding the box across his legs. The air in the attic had cleared some. A mockingbird began to sing from the big pecan outside the window. With his thumb and forefinger he opened the lid.

Inside was a manuscript written in a minute but regular hand, the words and lines cramped together. It was old. It was French. He no longer heard the bird's song or felt the heat or smelled the grass he had cut early that morning; instead, he imagined he could hear his heart beating and the blood rushing through his head. He turned away from the box and looked out the window. He saw the bird, its throat swelling, and heard the song, note after note, filling the thick air. He turned back to the manuscript.

He reached for the topmost page but drew his hand back, fearing the paper might turn to dust beneath his touch. He sat and studied the tiny, convoluted script. But he was unable to make any sense of it because of the size of the writing, only read the title: *La Veritable Historie du Duc Octavius Maury, de L'Esclavage À Son Évasion*. The name Maury was a familiar one. That was the name of one of his tennis partners, a common surname in the county.

Robert knew of Octavius Maury's connection to the house. He was a slave who had escaped from the plantation in the 1840s. He killed his master Strode Maury and then went down the river to the Gulf. Legend had it that he sailed a small boat to Haiti.

After the war was over Octavius, calling himself a duke, had appeared at the house—a house saved from the torch only because it had been used as a regimental headquarters and the Yankee general had developed an affection for it—and bought it. Then, he disappeared, went to Paris to buy furnishings, but died there of some disease, and the house and land were sold to the previous owners, who had made money in timber after the war.

Robert took a deep breath and carefully lifted the topmost sheet. The paper was thick and supple in his hands. Octavius had written on both sides of the page. Octavius, who had to have gone to some expense and trouble to obtain such paper, must have assumed what he was writing was a permanent record. He had sealed the box to protect the contents from the ravages of insects and the Mississippi humidity. Robert took the manuscript downstairs.

He sat at the kitchen table with a magnifying glass and began to struggle with the first sentence. But as he puzzled out the letters, he put down the glass. He looked out across the yard toward where it dropped away down to the river.

The troubadour's letters could wait. He would translate this memoir. He would retrace Ocatavius' journey to the Gulf. He would read the narrative on the river, the highway Octavius used to make his escape. Perhaps he might buy a small boat in Gulfport and sail it to Haiti, but it was the romance of the river journey that appealed the most to him. He settled the matter in his mind. He would not look at the manuscript until he was on the river.

He walked out across the yard beneath the oaks and pecans. The treetops were loud with cicadas. He felt the vibration of the sound against his body. He looked up into the trees and imagined the insects: thin legs, black eyes, greenish backs. Then he was at the river.

The river swung by below with a sluggish current, gray snags like the bleached bones of some huge animal protruding from the brown water. It was going to be shoals and sandbars all the way to the Gulf. He tried to imagine what it had been like for Octavius, alone and hunted, with freedom an impossible distance away as he moved through that wilderness. Robert would be able to experience only the river, the movement between one point on the map and another, the leisurely drift toward the Gulf, but none of the fear. And there would be no wilderness, only the illusion of one created by that thin screen of trees between the river and the pine tree farms and cultivated fields.

He listened to the suck of the current against the snags; he smelled the stink of the river mud; he looked into the trees on the far bank and focused on a single leaf outlined against the blue sky. He ached to be on the water.

Chapter Two

HENRY MAURY'S CAR came slowly up the driveway. Henry taught biology at the state university. Robert's tennis partners knew nothing of the murder of Elaine, and he felt no inclination to tell them. Henry's research was concentrated on a rare type of grass, which grew in only a few places in the Mississippi Delta. One day Henry explained the nature of the research to Robert, who did not quite understand. Henry was a practical scientist, comfortable in his straightforward view of the world. For Henry nothing was permanently hidden. Everything had a possible explanation.

Robert had met Henry at a tournament in Jackson, along with the two other members of their foursome. In July they had started playing in the morning to avoid the heat. Henry was usually early.

Henry, whose skin was the color of a crow's wing, came into the house. Robert showed him the manuscript.

"Was Octavius Maury kin to you?" Robert asked.

Henry shook his head. "My ancestors were slaves on his land, but I'm no kin to Octavius."

As Henry examined the first page, he found himself wondering if Robert were the right person to do the translation. It should be in the hands of some translator of color. Then he felt embarrassed for thinking something like that.

"French, you can read it easy."

"Yes, but it's difficult to make out the words. Everything's all

7

run together."

The other players arrived.

Paul taught at the county elementary school. He was a small, gentle man with curly brown hair. He and Robert were doubles partners. Robert was a tall man with a big serve. He provided the power, Paul the quickness and touch. Paul was a fierce competitor, but unlike the rest of them he had sympathy for his opponents. For Paul a match never became a personal struggle. Once, when an angry opponent tried to take his head off with an overhead, Paul simply smiled and said "bad luck." Paul was one of the few people Robert had ever met whom he could without hesitation call good.

Paul spent his summers playing tennis and reading. He liked stories full of magic. This summer he was reading E.T.A. Hoffman. He had immersed himself in a book between matches when he and Robert had played doubles in a tournament in Natchez the week before. Sometimes Robert wondered what Paul saw when he looked at the world. If Henry and Paul both were looking at a big pecan in Robert's front yard, Robert suspected that Henry saw an array of physical forces at work, things he could measure. But Paul was a Druid. He read moral lessons in the shapes of the leaves, in the thrust of the tree towards the sky.

Mason worked only sporadically at odd jobs. He came from a poor family and had dropped out of the community college where he had gone to learn to care for golf courses. Mason carried a sort of permanent rage within him that Robert found unsettling. Tennis was an equalizer. Although the others were careful not to start discussions about books after matches, instead speaking of sports or women while Mason was present, Robert suspected that their very existence rankled Mason.

Robert never liked playing with Mason as a partner. Mason was given to fits of rage on the court. Once Robert watched him sit on a bench during a change-over and rip a towel into shreds. He was short like Paul but stocky instead of frail looking. He had big forearms and a good left-handed slice serve to the ad court. He was a redhead whose pale freckled skin was always burned and peeling.

They gathered around the table to look at the manuscript. Mason wondered if it was worth anything.

Robert picked up one of the pages and felt the weight of the paper. "No much. Octavius Maury wasn't an important historical figure."

They began to discuss how long it had taken him to reach Haiti. All of them agreed it would have taken several months. Just the trip to the Gulf must have been one of a number of weeks.

"I'm going down the river," Robert said. "Just like him. I'll translate the manuscript as I go. I'll live like he must have lived. Who's going with me?"

"I will," Henry said. "Just to the Gulf. Lucy and the kids will be visiting her mother next week. She never likes me to go with her. I'm working on a paper, but the world can wait for another paper on grass."

Henry thought of his ancestors working the plantation. Some who had tried to escape had been hunted down before they had traveled twenty miles. One, Samuel, had gotten as far as Virginia where he had been betrayed. Henry found himself wishing he were going on this trip with some of his kin instead of these white men. He suspected that in his heart Mason disliked black people. *Maybe that's it*, Henry thought. *It's just Mason. If he weren't going I'd be fine about it.*

"I'm on," Mason said. "It beats killing trees."

Mason had showed them the tool he used to inject poison into unwanted hardwoods for a company that raised pines for pulpwood.

"Too many snakes. I'm always stepping on a snake. Yesterday I got a big rattler with it. He tried to bite me, but I bit him instead. I've been thinking about quitting anyhow."

Mason was single. He lived in a trailer with his mother and grandmother, both of whom drew disability checks from Social Security. He drank up and gambled away much of his paycheck, if he happened to be working, and borrowed money from his kin too, never considering what the next day might bring. The only thing he paid any attention to was the tournament schedule and what his state ranking was going to be.

Sometimes Mason suspected the others thought they were better than him because he had not even completed high school. They were always talking about books they had read. He wondered if any of them would come home at night and read if they had spent all of a hot summer's day killing trees. His uncle had asked him why he was playing tennis with that "nigger." And that made him think that while he was out killing trees all day the blacks were sitting on their porches, drinking beer and taking it easy. But Henry was a university professor. Mason had never known a university professor until he met Henry and Robert. If Mason had had the inclination to think deeply about his relationship with Henry, he might have realized that he regarded him as someone who was neither white nor black.

"Paul?" Robert asked.

"I'll have to talk to Elizabeth," Paul said. "Once, some of my friends took canoes down the Mississippi to New Orleans. I couldn't go. I'd broken my arm. The Pearl's not the Mississippi, but I reckon it'll do."

Paul and Elizabeth lived in a house they had built with their own hands. They had acquired a pack of dogs, unable to turn away any stray that wandered up to the house set in the middle of forty acres of hardwoods. In their baseball caps, jeans, and running shoes the two looked like twins. Mason made fun of their dogs, saying he would come over and shoot a few anytime they wanted.

Paul suspected that Mason's attempts to be funny were grounded in his general rage at the world. He had students like Mason who came from poor white families. Occasionally he had been able to turn that rage into something positive. And things were changing. Children who grew up poor were going off to the university and escaping life at some plant or mill job. But Paul saw no way out for Mason.

They agreed they would leave in a week, right after the Fourth of July.

"We'll live off the land," Robert said. "Just like Octavius. We'll hunt and fish."

"And steal a few watermelons," Mason added.

Robert said he would buy a couple of johnboats and outboard motors.

They all agreed to make lists and later meet to compare them and produce a master list of provisions. Then they went out to play tennis.

After the match was over and they were gone, Robert got another beer from the refrigerator and sat on the porch where it was cool and comfortable. A breeze came up from the river, rustling the leaves in the pecans. He drank the beer carefully and then stretched out on the swing and slept.

Chapter Three

THE SUN ROSE, hanging suspended in the tops of the cypresses, as the men carried the two twenty-foot johnboats from the plantation shop to the edge of the bluff. Patches of mist lay on the dark water, held between the insect-loud riverbank scrims of trees. A pair of wood ducks approached from the opposite bank and, seeing the men and the boats, swung high and wide, circling back across the river to drop down into the swamp.

Once there had been huge cypress swamps along the river and a great longleaf pine forest, the home of panthers and bears and the Chickasaw nation, that stretched all the way to the Gulf. Now most of the stands of cypress were gone, along with the pines, the longleaf trees reduced to a few patches of national forest and the swamps to a narrow band along the river. The Chickasaws had been the first to go.

When he was on the river, Robert liked to imagine he was in the country before the first white man arrived or even the first Indian. He felt he had touched something of the old wilderness, a place where men and animals and the river and the great forest had existed together in measured stately dignity. But the spell was always broken by the sound of a plane passing overhead or a train whistle or the clatter of an outboard motor.

They used ropes to lower the boats. The flat-bottomed boats, which drew only a few inches of water, were necessary on the shallow river, full of shoals and sandbars. Robert and Henry had welded frames for canopies amidships.

They installed the two outboards. They stretched canvas over the frames. They loaded gasoline and tents. They brought a tent for each man. The tents, designed for tropical weather, were mostly mosquito netting with a rain fly that could be pulled up if necessary. Robert was looking forward to lying in the tent and looking up at the stars. They brought cooking gear, fishing tackle, guns, two cast nets, rope, lanterns and fuel, plastic water jugs, and water purification filters. By now the sun was well up. It was already hot.

Henry packed cameras and guides for the identification of plants, insects, birds, and fish. He brought field glasses, a magnifying glass, and sketch pads.

Mason wore a white polyester shirt and pants designed for bone fishing in the Florida Keys, and a pith helmet. He said he feared that without protection he would burn so badly he would have to get off the river. He was in charge of the topographic maps, which he had laminated in plastic to protect them from the water. He had packed a jar of his cousin's homemade barbecue sauce. He said he planned to eat barbecued gator tail before the trip was over. He brought half a case of whiskey.

Paul filled a waterproof bag with books. He knew something of engines and had prepared a tool kit with spare sparkplugs and shear pins. He was the only one who was not armed. He had never shot a gun. He had agreed to fish but not to hunt. But he was concerned about how he would feel about being involved in the shooting of game. He and Elizabeth regularly ate venison friends gave them. So it seemed to him that he should feel no differently about the game he ate on the trip.

Robert had made enlarged photocopies of the manuscript, which was still difficult to read, but at least with photocopies he would not have to use a magnifying glass. He packed the manuscript and his dictionaries in a waterproof bag. He carried a .270 Mannlicher, a bow, and a shotgun.

Scott Ely

Robert and Henry took one boat, Paul and Mason the other.

The men took up the ash poles Henry and Robert had cut and planed in the plantation shop. They would pole the boats. Here it was too shallow and snag-ridden for the motors.

They drifted by the sandbar and down through the shoal. Then the river made a bend, and they entered a world that contained nothing but trees and brown water and blue sky. Robert took a deep breath, sucking in the smell of the water and the mud and the trees and a faint hint of something dead. They floated by poplar and water birch and stands of cypress.

They surprised a big white wading bird, which took flight and flapped ungainly away downstream.

"I wouldn't want to eat that thing," Mason said. "But that might be all we'll get. We just missed our chance."

Mason unfolded the map and studied it. He liked being in charge of navigation, something he was certain he could do better than his schoolteacher companions.

Robert, who sat under the canopy of the lead boat, removed the manuscript from the waterproof bag. For a long time he sat there, wondering if attempting a translation while floating down the river was a good idea. He worked through the first sentence, turning the possibilities over and over in his mind, trying to guess at what Octavius' intention might have been.

Here and there were milk cartons, used by cat fishermen to mark their lines, floating on the water. But they saw no one.

Henry opened a bird book and located the big wading bird. He identified it as a great white heron.

"That thing eats nothing but fish and frogs," Robert said. "It'd taste of fish. Anyone sing out if you see something we can eat."

Henry took a book out of his bag. "What about snakes? You get hungry enough you'll eat one and like it." He held the book up for Mason to see and showed him a few of the color plates, reciting the names of the snakes. "All of these are good to eat."

"I don't care how hungry I get," Mason said. "I ain't eating a snake."

14

Henry took pictures of Robert and the other boat. Then he attached a telephoto lens to the camera and waited for some animal to appear on the river.

As they drifted around a bend, a dead tree full of vultures came into view.

Henry took pictures of the vultures, big birds with red heads and dark feathers. One flew off but the others remained as they passed, the birds turning their necks to watch the men.

Paul had not taken his eyes off the birds. Another bird launched itself from the tree, flapping its wings to gain altitude. Then it sailed with fixed wings in circles over the river, just above the treetops. Its wings trembled slightly as it hit a thermal rising from a sandbar. It made a turn and rose with the column of air.

"Beautiful," Paul said.

"Nothing beautiful about a buzzard," Mason observed.

"I mean they're graceful in flight."

"I think they're ugly all the time."

Robert put down the manuscript and watched them too. "Only Paul could love a vulture."

The vulture sailed over them, turning above the trees.

"We've got to watch for game," Henry said. "It can't be herons or vultures. We're not that hungry yet. Keep your eyes open."

Mason and Paul dropped behind the other boat.

Not long after, a rifle shot rang out, the sound elongated by the tree-covered banks. A vulture toppled out of the tree, spiraling down, vainly trying to fly with a broken wing. Robert turned to see Mason grinning.

"Barbecued buzzard for lunch," Mason said.

"What'd you do that for?" Paul cried.

"Some of the best eating I've had was buzzard. You just got to cook'em right."

Mason returned the rifle to its case.

"Aren't you going to go get it?" Paul asked.

Mason looked up at the bank. "It's thick up there. Probably full of cottonmouths."

"It's still alive."

"It'll be dead soon. I never saw nobody so worried about a buzzard."

Paul slipped over the side and into the waist-deep water. The bottom was mud instead of sand, and it sucked at his feet. He planned to kill the bird if it were still alive. It suddenly struck him that he had never killed anything. He had brought nothing with him to do the job. He hoped the bird was already dead.

"We can't spend all day waiting for you to find that bird," Mason called out.

"Let him go," Robert said.

Paul reached the bank and worked his way up the side.

"He's gonna get himself bit by a snake," Mason warned.

Paul disappeared into the underbrush. They hugged the bank in a spot of shade and waited for his return.

Paul made his way around the edge of a clump of briars. He hoped the bird had not fallen there. Then he saw it, standing on the ground with one wing spread and the other dangling uselessly. The bird raised its head and fluffed out its feathers. It hissed at him and clacked its beak.

When he took a step toward it, the bird ran from him with its hopping, ungainly gait. Paul followed and cornered the bird against the briars. It turned to face him and hissed and clacked its beak again. He suddenly realized that he had no intention of killing the bird.

Then he slowly backed the bird up into the briars. When the bird got its good wing entangled in the vines, Paul made a dive for it. He went for the beak, knowing that was what could hurt him. He got one hand around the beak and grabbed the good wing with the other, folding the wing up against the bird's body.

He expected the bird to smell bad, but it did not. It just smelled like a bird, no different from a large parrot one of his friends owned. He looked into the bird's dark eye, an eye that could spot a dead rabbit from miles away, and saw himself reflected there.

To free up the hand he was using to keep the beak closed, he tied the beak shut with the neoprene strap that secured his sunglasses. He started back for the river, carrying the bird in his arms. It was still now and had ceased to hiss or puff out its feathers. It was amazingly light in his arms for its size.

They heard him coming down the bank.

Mason stood up to urinate over the side of the boat. "Went to all that trouble to wring a buzzard's neck."

Paul came down through a cane thicket. They could not see him yet, but they could hear him and see the cane moving. He cried out. The cane rattled as he fell down the bank and slid feet first into the river. He held the vulture to his chest, one hand around its featherless neck and his arm around on its body. The bird flapped its good wing.

"What's he gonna do with that thing?" Mason asked.

"You said we could barbecue it," Henry observed.

"Not even my cousin's best sauce could make that meat taste good."

Paul waded to his boat, holding the vulture against his chest with one hand and restraining the bird's good wing with the other. He put the bird into the boat. Henry was looking up the bird in one of his books.

"I'll splint its wing," Paul said. "I'll release it when it's well."

"You don't have to worry about that beak," Henry said. "That's a turkey vulture, *Cathartes aura*. Its beak is not that strong. It's designed for eating rotten meat. Its name means "pacifier" or "cleanser." The Cherokee called it the "peace eagle" because in flight it resembles an eagle but doesn't kill. It hunts by both sight and smell. Eats vegetable things as much as it eats meat. It's a clean bird. Spends several hours a day preening and washing itself. And listen to this. It cleanses carrion by passing it though its guts. Its droppings are bacteria free."

Paul and Henry splinted the bird's wing. Paul tied a cord around one of its legs and made a perch in the boat out of a sapling. The bird calmed down and sat on the perch without attempting to flap its good wing.

"A bird that eats dead things has to stink," Mason said.

"And I thought you had no imagination?" Paul said. "It just smells like a bird to me."

"What's he mean that I've got no imagination?" Mason asked.

Robert and Henry did not reply.

"Nothing," Paul said. "I was just kidding. You know, like you kid me about my dogs."

This seemed to satisfy Mason.

They poled the boats out into the current and went down the river.

Robert dipped his straw hat in the river to keep his head cool and drank from a water bottle. They had brought several water jugs of cold water. Soon that would be gone, and they would take all their water from the river. Pumped through ceramic filters and into the jugs, the water would be safe to drink but warm as their urine.

Now the river widened and deepened some, but not enough to use the motors. The water was clear and filled with schools of suckers.

"Turtles," Henry said.

Robert looked downriver. He saw nothing. Henry was pulling off his t-shirt. Except for Mason, they all wore swimming trunks and river sandals.

"Where?" Paul asked.

Henry pointed to the water just ahead of the boat. "Soft shells. Our dinner."

They passed over a whole group of small turtles lying buried in the sand, their long, tube-like necks rising off the bottom of the river like a colony of snakes.

Henry put on a skin-diver's mask and snorkel and a pair of flippers.

"You keep the boat a little behind me," Henry said. "They lying on the bottom. They think as long as they stay still no one can see'em."

Henry went over the side into the clear, waist-deep water.

18

Robert watched Henry drift along, the tips of his flippers brushing the bow every now and then. Finally Henry came upon a large turtle whose thick neck protruded from the bottom of the river. He raised his hand for the boats to stop. Then he dived on the turtle, approaching it from behind.

He moved his hand toward the turtle's neck and cautiously slipped his fingers around it. Quickly he closed his fingers, applying a choke-hold to the turtle. Immediately the turtle exploded from the sand, raising a cloud of sediment, and began to thrash its feet in an attempt to swim away.

"He'll have to hold on tight," Mason said. "That turtle'll try to draw in its head. A big one's hard to hold."

The turtle attempted to twist its head to bite Henry, but Henry tightened his grip. Then it tried to swim away from him, its weight and struggles rolling Henry over so he was lying on the sand, the leathery carapace pressed against his chest. It was as if Henry and the turtle were joined together.

"He'll be running out of air," Paul said.

Henry gained his feet and stood up, the water cascading from his body, while he held the turtle in a desperate embrace. The big turtle treaded air, churning its legs furiously.

Robert maneuvered the boat to him. They put the turtle into the live well. As Robert stroked the turtle's leathery back, he wondered how old it was. Its ancestors had swum in the river when Octavius had passed this way. The turtle's webbed feet made scratching sounds against the plastic walls.

"Octavius write about catching turtles?" Henry asked Robert.

"You'll have to wait and see."

Robert was pleased with the way the trip was going. The river was filled with food. All they had to do was harvest it. They decided to eat the turtle at the evening meal.

At noon they stopped on a sandbar to eat dried apricots, cheese, crackers, and sardines. They sat under a tarp rigged near the water's edge. Getting too close to the underbrush on the banks exposed them to mosquitoes.

Paul named the vulture Hoffman. He took the bird down to the foot of the sandbar to a patch of shade cast by a magnolia. There he persuaded the bird to take a perch on a driftwood log. He offered the bird a sardine, but Hoffman refused to eat.

Mason wandered over to watch. "You might as well shoot him. He'll never eat."

"Hoffman *will* fly again." At Paul's words, Hoffman hissed at Mason, who took a step backwards. "One of these days, he might be flying over you, sizing you up for a meal."

"That bird'll never fly."

"He *will* eat. He will *fly*. Now leave us alone."

Mason joined Henry and Robert. They lolled about under the tarp and watched Paul. He talked to the bird, which perched on the log and regarded him gravely, every now and then stretching out his good wing or turning his head. They were too far away to understand what Paul was saying. Henry quickly tired of watching Paul and the bird and dropped off to sleep.

"I don't believe that bird can't hurt you with his beak," Mason said. "I hope I don't miss him chopping off one of Paul's fingers. He'll do it too. You just wait and see."

Paul reached out his hand toward the vulture, all the while talking to the bird.

"What do you think he's saying?" Mason asked.

"Just talking him calm."

"Looks like he's singing to me."

"I don't think so."

"Lullabies for a buzzard. I never thought I'd see something like that."

Henry sat up. "Not much chance of a man sleeping with you two around."

Henry took a fine seine and went to collect aquatic insects. He stood at mid-river, examining them through a magnifying glass. He put the collecting net on a log and made sketches.

Robert considered returning to the translation but decided he would wait until they were on the water again. He lay down to sleep. Just before he drifted off, he heard Henry come under the tarp. Henry and Mason talked for a time until Henry told Mason he wanted to go to sleep. Mason devoted his time to watching Paul watch the vulture. Paul had his back to Mason, but Hoffman was looking directly at the tarp. The vulture pulled himself up to his full height and puffed out his feathers. Paul never moved. Then Mason grew bored and lay down and soon dropped off to sleep.

Hoffman turned his head to the side and regarded Paul with one eye. Then the bird appeared to be looking at men under the tarp. Paul wondered if the vulture could tell the difference between a sleeping man and a dead man.

"What do you see?" Paul asked.

As if in reply Hoffman stretched out his good wing.

Paul knew one thing for certain. The vulture wanted to be up in the sky, sailing effortlessly over the river and swamps. Paul felt sleepy. He wrapped the end of the cord about his hand and lay down and slept.

FIRST THE MEN under the tarp woke. Henry went to wake Paul. But before he could reach him, Paul was awakened by Hoffman clacking his beak at Henry's approach. They returned to the river.

"Tonight I want turtle steaks with tomatoes and corn," Robert said. "Let's keep on the lookout for gardens."

From time to time they hit a section of the river where it was possible to use the motors. They enjoyed the breeze on their faces.

The banks were mostly wooded, but occasionally they came upon pastureland. Once there were cattle in the river, standing in the water up to their necks. They steered the boat carefully between them. One of the steers bellowed but none of them moved. They stood motionless, twitching their ears at the passage of the boats.

Then they all heard the sound of an engine. At first they thought it was a boat coming up river. But Henry recognized it as a pump. Someone was pumping water up from the river for irrigation.

"My tomatoes," Robert said.

"Most likely corn," Henry observed.

A farmer might be growing corn for hogs or for sale, but often Robert knew that he might grow a few vegetables for his own use.

Henry turned out to be right. Someone was irrigating a cornfield. They could see the stalks for the boats. They took the boat down below the field, and while Robert and Henry stayed with the boats, Mason and Paul walked back up to it. They soon returned with corn and okra and tomatoes.

Downriver a few miles they made camp at a big bend. There was a low white bluff on one side and a large sandbar on the other. After they beached the boats, they set up the tarp, deciding to wait until it cooled off in the evening to eat. Paul made a portable perch for Hoffman out of willow poles he lashed together. He brought the bird under the tarp with them.

"That thing stinks," Mason said.

"It'd be hard for anything to smell worse than us," Henry pointed out.

That silenced Mason and he, along with Paul and Henry, lay down to sleep. But Hoffman did not sleep. He cocked his head to one side and cast his eye on Robert. His steady gaze made Robert a little uncomfortable. But soon he was caught up in the translation and forgot Hoffman was there.

He finally reached the end of the first section. He returned the manuscript to its waterproof bag and lay down and closed his eyes. As he waited for sleep, he heard Octavius' words in his ears, as persistent and powerful as the suck of the river on the bluff.

Chapter Four

ROBERT WOKE AND looked out over the river. It was still illuminated by the sun, which had fallen low over the big timber behind them. The face of the bluff sparkled, the light reflecting off some mineral in the clay. The other men were asleep. He went down to the river and swam. Then he gathered driftwood and laid a fire but did not start it. He sat on the sand and watched swallows flying low over the water, dropping down from time to time to drink. He imagined Octavius passing by this spot, trying to put as much distance as possible between himself and his murdered master. And he imagined him holding Haiti, the idea of freedom, constantly in his mind to keep down the panic, the despair he must have felt, as he contemplated the task of making his way down the river and attempting a sea voyage in a small boat.

At dusk the men woke and swam in the river. Robert lit the fire, the sparks shooting up into the half-darkened sky. The moon rose over the bluff.

"When do we hear about Octavius?" Henry asked.

"After we eat," he said.

They sat around the fire and drank Mason's whiskey.

"I'd trade all this whiskey for one cold beer," Mason said. "When we hit the Georgetown bridge, I'm walking into town for a six-pack."

They all agreed that a cold beer would be good.

After the fire burned down to coals, Henry butchered the turtle.

Paul offered both meat and entrails to Hoffman, who refused to eat. Mason had quit complaining the bird stank, finally conceding that Hoffman smelled almost exactly like one of his aunt's yard chickens.

"Henry, do vultures eat every day?" Paul asked.

Henry was washing his hands. "I don't know."

"That buzzard likes his meat ripe," Mason said. "He'd turn his nose up at anything that ain't been dead a few days." Mason paused and looked at Paul. "What you been saying to that bird?"

"Whatever's in my head. I want him to get used to the sound of my voice."

Paul offered Hoffman some water. The bird refused to drink.

"That bird don't want this turtle, but I do," Mason said. "Let's get moving with supper."

Paul and Mason wrapped ears of corn in foil and put them on the coals. Then Henry cut the turtle meat into thick steaks and laid them on a grill he set over the coals. Robert fried the okra in an iron skillet. Paul sliced the tomatoes.

They ate the steaks and drank more whiskey. A whippoorwill began to call from across the river; a fish jumped. The night was still and warm.

"Read it to us," Henry said.

Mason built up the fire, and Paul lit a gasoline lantern. Hoffman put his head under his good wing and went to sleep. Robert took up the manuscript.

He began to read.

A True Relation of the Escape from Slavery of Duke Octavius Maury

Preface

*I write this narrative to record precisely what
I have done, those manifold crimes I have com-*

mitted and those committed against me; but I do not write in a vain attempt to mitigate my guilt to man or God (although what I have done seems likely to have damned me many times over); I write so I can front this thing clearly, which oftentimes sends me evil dreams and lies upon me as some damned incubus; so that I feel myself to be smothered. God help me and those I have wronged and those who have wronged me. I intend to give a simple, clear account of it all; so I may gain something; but I must confess I know not what.

Mississippi 1868

My Escape

Strode Maury promised me Paris and freedom, but I came to realize he would give me neither, that I would have to take my freedom if I wanted it. We had gone to the hunting cabin on the river. There we hunted and fished and read the English poets. He had secretly taught me to read and write English. And to speak and write and read French. At the cabin we would often speak nothing but French to each other, to prepare for that time in Paris when together we would wander about that great shining city.

And love. He taught me about love. I was sixteen when he bought me, he already a man of twenty-five. For five years I knew nothing but him and his body, the scars on his thigh and right arm from pistol balls. And a long scar on his chest from a Bowie knife. He told me he was enamored of my blackness, no trace of white blood

*in me. He said holding me in his arms was like
embracing Africa or a moonless night in the
middle of a Mississippi summer. I loved his
words. He was a hot-tempered man and had
fought many duels. I dressed him every morning. When I was eighteen, I began wearing his
clothes, the fine linen and silk garments brought
with those crops of cotton he planted on the rich
bottomland. He began to dress himself.*

*We went to the cabin—miles downriver from
the house and surrounded by that immense pri-
meval forest of pines, whose tops soughed in
breezes that came up from the Gulf a hundred
miles away—to be alone, for at the house there
were too many eyes and ears. There were no
women, the only other house servant an old man
he had taught to cook. All the slaves knew about
us. I imagined them laughing at me among themselves. Talking about us in secret, whispering it
in each other's ears, as they lay exhausted,
sweat-covered and stinking in their cabins from
a long day in the fields. Often I was at his side
when he rode out to oversee the work. I saw hate
in their eyes when they looked at me.*

*He was teaching me to use a sextant, the
same one he had used as a naval officer, when
he told me he was bringing a woman to the house.
He said it like that, simply a woman, and I
thought he had bought a slave who knew how to
cook. But that was not it at all. She was a white
woman from New Orleans, and she would be his
wife when she arrived at the big house. He spoke
of buying a piano for her and how fine it was
going to be to have music in the house. We would
listen to her play and sing in the evenings.*

We were standing in a field by the river. The cabin, built up on stilts against the high water, was behind us in a grove of live oaks. I thought it was not possible that the trees were still standing. It seemed to me that some cataclysmic event should occur: a fire, a flood, an earthquake. I screamed; I cried.

He put his arms around me and told me that at the birth of his first male child he would give me my freedom and a sum of money. I could go to Paris. I could go anywhere I wanted. When the woman arrived, I would return to dressing him, return to being his servant, but things between us would remain the same. I knew that nothing would be the same. I would never sleep in the big house with him again.

I asked him why. Did he love this woman as he loved me and I him? And he said that he needed heirs or the house and the land and crops were nothing. They would die when he died, no more substantial than if they had been made of air. It would go against his nature, but a woman was necessary for the future of his works.

It was then that I decided I would allow him to give me nothing. I would take my freedom. I knew of Haiti and the slave revolt. He had taught me navigation and how to sail, things he thought a gentleman should be able to do.

That evening, as was our custom, we bathed in the river and then ran together naked, a race I always won, to the cabin. We did this to avoid the mosquitoes, which descended in clouds upon us once we left the open air of the sandbar. We brushed the sand from our feet and entered the cabin, retreating to make love in the bed beneath mosquito netting.

I found it strange that my desire for him was even greater than it had ever been. Our bodies were hot from the run, with just a trace of the river's coolness left on our skin. I stretched myself out against him and tried not to think of the woman, of his betrayal. And I lost myself to the feel of him beneath my hands and to his caresses.

We slept. I woke and looked at him sleeping beside me. And the woman and what he was about to do all came flooding back into my mind. I took the Bowie knife he had given me on my last birthday and, caught like a limed bird in the grip of that bloody passion, I plunged it into his breast. He gave a great groan and he died.

I tried to pull the knife out, but it was immovable. Finally I put my knee on his chest and taking a good grip on the hilt pulled with both hands. The knife came free, and I fell to the floor. I sat there holding the knife, the sweet scent of blood filling the cabin. I took in great gulps of air; I felt faint. It was the intoxication of freedom, I told myself. I had loved this man and he said he loved me, but he had abandoned me at a moment's notice to a woman and his false belief that he could trick time with heirs; he had deluded himself that he, a mere man, could actually make something that would endure beyond a season.

Somewhere off between the cabin and the river a night bird was calling. To calm myself I sat there and counted the calls and gradually, as I approached a hundred, the pounding of my heart subsided, and I was tranquil.

I got up and worked quickly. I had only the

short summer's night. I wished that night could last for days, for weeks. I took the two rifles, two shotguns, and the boxed French dueling pistols he had been teaching me to use. We had shot buttons at the ends of strings from twenty paces; we had shot silver dollars out of each other's hands. I took bullet molds and lead and powder and patches. I took an ax and an adze and a sharpening stone. I took the sextant, a compass, a chronometer, and Bowditch's book on navigation, and charts of the Gulf. I took a smoked haunch of venison and flour and cornmeal and salt and an iron pot and skillet.

Once I had loaded the skiff, I rowed it out into the current. The river was a little high for July. I was thankful for that. Under moonlight and then starlight when the moon fell below the trees, I rowed. I heard no human sound from the big timber and saw no lights. I rowed on into that beautiful blackness of the moonless night.

When the sky lightened and the morning star appeared, I ran the boat up into the mouth of a creek and beached it on a little island inside a screen of willows so that anyone coming upon me would have to approach by water and would have little chance of seeing me until they were upon me. I had decided to travel only at night. Any white man I came upon would assume I was an escaped slave. If I claimed to be a free person of color, he would demand to see my papers.

If I were lucky the body of my master would not be discovered for a week or maybe even two. Sometimes we stayed at the cabin for as long as two weeks and saw no one, for in the summer there was little traffic on the river. From here to

*the Gulf there was nothing but pines, that track-
less expanse of forest inhabited by a few hunters and charcoal makers, who built conical kilns
in the forest. Several times a year they floated
their product down to the coast to sell or trade
for powder, shot, lead, and salt.*

*I checked the powder pans of both the rifles
and loaded the dueling pistols and stuck one in
my belt. Then I threw a piece of canvas over me
to protect myself from the mosquitoes and taking the second pistol in my hand lay down in the
bottom of the skiff and slept.*

No one said anything. The whippoorwills called; the gasoline
lantern hissed.

Robert found himself more stunned by his reading of Octavius'
matter-of-fact account of the murder than he had been during the
process of translation. For a moment he could hear the police officer in Africa telling him what he knew about the murder of Elaine.
Then Robert found himself remembering research his teacher had
done on the troubadours. His teacher Peter Strauss had met a violent end, found murdered in a cornfield in a rural area of south-
west France. Two of Peter's childhood friends had become involved
in black market antiquities. A deal had gone bad in Africa, a son of
the country's dictator had died, and killers had tracked them to
France to take revenge. But in the end Peter, who had been in love
with his friend's wife all his life, had been the only one who had
died. Peter had told Robert about his love for Cassie many times.
Robert always wondered about Peter's willingness to talk about
intimate details of his personal life. It was something Robert would
have never done.

Peter had gone to France not in pursuit of Cassie but to do
research on a new troubadour poet he had discovered, Bertran de
Fanjeaux. He had been invited by Cassie, with whom he had had a
correspondence over the years, to visit her and her husband

Rembert. Bertran had been murdered by one of the counts of Toulouse and the story of his death was told in a document written by a monk who lived a hundred years later. Poems that Bertran had written were contained in something called *The White Book*. Peter had gone to France to search for the book or a copy of it, but he never found it.

He remembered the day in Peter's office, just before he left for France, when Peter told him about the monk's account. They had also talked about Cassie. He was thinking about not visiting her at all. He had not seen her in thirty years. Robert could hear Peter's voice, his soft Mississippi Delta accent, as he told him the story.

"Bertran fell in love with the wife of one of the counts of Toulouse. He loved her according to the ideals presented in troubadour poetry. But then he abandoned these ideals and they became lovers.

"Her husband discovered erotic poems Bertran sent to his wife. Written after the manner of Sextus Propertius. The count had copies made of the poems. Soon the spies he set on them revealed that they were truly lovers. The count plotted a terrible revenge.

"He sent Bertran on a mission to Barcelona where he was intercepted and killed on the road. His body was cooked along with a lamb and served to his wife and her attendants while the count was away. Usually the way these stories work is that immediately after the meal the person taking the revenge explains to his victim exactly what was served. But his one is different. The count said nothing to his wife, who still thought Bertran was in Barcelona. She waited every day for some letter or news of him.

"The count had Bertran skinned. The skin was then sent to an expert tanner and then to a bookmaker who used the skin to bind a book of Bertran's erotic poems. According to the account I found, the leather made of the skin was said to be the same color as new snow. No doubt an exaggeration.

"The count waited until he gave a great feast near the end of the year and presented the book to his wife as a gift. The great hall was filled with people. There were large fires burning, for it was bitterly cold outside.

"She ran her hands over the book, exclaiming as she did at the quality of the leather. Then she opened it and there was one of Bertran's poems. The count whispered in her ear that a few months before she and her attendants—who he also held responsible, for they all knew of the affair—had eaten her lover.

"The lady ran screaming from the hall, her attendants following in amazement. She ran to the top of the chateau's tallest tower and threw herself onto the stones below. The count had all her attendants tossed into a huge pit filled with burning logs."

Peter did not think he was going to find the actual white book, but he did hope to find some of the poems contained in it.

Then their conversation turned back to Cassie again. Robert had been struck by how uncertain Peter was about seeing Cassie. He remembered supposing at the time that Peter had idealized her all those years, and now he knew that the woman he was going to see would not be the girl he had fallen in love with when he was a boy.

"He killed his lover just like that," Paul said.

Henry stood up and walked in a circle about the fire. "What choice did he have?" *Embracing Africa.* The two groups, masters and slaves, were hopelessly entangled, the one morally destroyed and the other abject in their loss of freedom. He had made a conscious effort not to think about his past, about his ancestors who worked on the land surrounding Robert's house. He liked the rigorous laws of scientific investigation. He detested ambiguity. But he supposed that in the end ambiguity was the only hope, when the races had so mixed themselves that it would be impossible by sight to determine with perfect certitude someone's ancestry.

"You all right, Henry?" Robert asked.

"I'm fine," Henry said. "It's just such a powerful story. It speaks to me."

He sat down again.

"He wasn't looking for freedom," Paul said. "He was jealous.

He wanted to be free, but he wanted that love to go on and on. In Paris. I wish he hadn't killed Strode Maury. I understand why he did it. I guess I don't know what I'd have done. Maybe he knew unconsciously that killing Strode was the only way he could truly be free. Oh, I guess I don't really know what I'm saying. If he just hadn't done it."

Paul tried to imagine himself in Octavius' position. He wondered if he could have actually killed someone in such an intimate fashion. Octavius *felt* Strode Maury's flesh give way under the knife. There was the smell of blood. Paul thought that he might be able to kill someone (only if that person was threatening his life or Elizabeth's), with a rifle or pistol but not with a knife.

Mason took up a stick from the fire and jabbed the burning end of it into the sand. "Paul would've stuck him with that knife." Paul's "goodness" drove Mason wild. All of them: Robert and Paul and Henry could afford the luxury of being good. But Mason believed they acted in that fashion only when it was convenient. None of them had to work at a job they hated just to pay rent on a trailer, just to buy a few groceries. Mason had had to endure insults from the men at the Avery Creek Social Club, a beer joint that functioned as a private club so black people could be excluded, over his playing tennis with "that nigger professor." Lately Mason had found himself defending Henry and that had made him uneasy. He wondered if he would tell the members of the club the story of Octavius and Strode Maury.

"Don't assume everyone would do what you'd do," Paul said.

"He was backed into a corner," Robert said. "There was nothing else he could do."

A clear image of Elaine lying in the rainforest appeared before him. She lay face down; she was wearing a blue back pack. He had brought that back pack home from Africa. It was in the top of a closet at their house. He imagined himself lying down beside her. He turned her over as if they were in their bed at home and pulled her close to make love to her. But when her face came into view, he saw the bullet hole just above her left eye. There was no blood.

Then that waking daydream suddenly vanished as if he had been wakened suddenly and violently from a nightmare. He felt cold. He took a deep breath to calm himself and looked at the faces of his companions. They were waiting for him to speak, but it was clear they had not the slightest inkling of what he had just experienced.

Robert continued. "I guess I'm wondering what I'd have done if I were in his place. But I'm having a hard time imagining myself killing anyone. It wasn't like a soldier killing an anonymous enemy. He was killing his lover, someone he knew the taste and smell of. It couldn't have been easy to do that.

"And I'm struck with all those details, the list of things he took with him. It's like those details were a way of keeping the enormity of what he'd done at bay."

Robert paused. For some reason he wanted a cigarette. He had not smoked in years.

"What else? Yes, it's already made going down this river different for me. He was *here*. He's killed Strode and he's just going to forget about him, put him off in some inaccessible place in his mind."

And as he spoke the words he considered how he had reacted to the death of Elaine. *I loved her*, he thought. *I loved her*. At his moment he considered telling his companions everything. But it did not seem possible to him to speak of love before Mason.

Henry picked up Mason's map case and handed it to him. "And he eluded his pursuers. He reached Haiti. That's a miracle of small boat navigation. Tell us where you think he is." Mason's ability with the maps had surprised Henry. It seemed to him that Mason might do well in one of his classes. But still he would have preferred that Mason had not come on the trip. Henry wondered if it was Mason's anger and not his probable racism that disturbed him the most. Henry had been careful not to fall victim to anger.

Mason got out his maps and tried to decide which of the numerous creeks Octavius had run the skiff up into. But he could never make up his mind how much river Octavius had covered that first night. He told them that they had not even reached Octavius' starting place yet. Tomorrow they would surely pass it.

Hoffman took his head out from under his wing and stretched out the good wing as if he were preparing to fly. Paul decided he would watch Hoffman tame, the method falconers used to tame birds of prey. He would outlast the bird. He would not sleep until Hoffman took meat from his hand. The others were still talking about Octavius. Robert, who had just finished reading a passage, sat with the manuscript in his hands.

". . . So you see, by killing he diminished himself," Henry said. "He knew the consequences of what he'd done."

"You'd rather he'd stayed?" Mason asked.

"No, but you all heard. He *knew*."

"I want to hear what happens when he meets his first woman. I wonder if he ever had a woman. I mean before he escaped."

So they sat around for some time, speculating on what Octavius might know about women. And each of them imagined that he knew something about women.

Paul walked over to a stand of willows and cut a switch. Then he moved Hoffman's perch just outside the circle of firelight. He took some turtle meat back to Hoffman.

They watched as he offered a piece to the vulture. The bird turned his head away.

"Wasting his time," Mason said.

"Don't be so sure," Robert said. "Paul looks determined."

Paul murmured something to the bird. Than all was quiet again. The insects whined from the trees. Night birds called.

Mason and Robert went off to sleep. Paul sat by Hoffman's perch, a bowl of turtle meat beside him. Every time Hoffman tried to put his head under his wing, Paul prodded him awake with the switch.

Henry walked over to where Paul sat before the bird.

"You're going to watch him tame?" Henry asked.

"If I don't he'll die," Paul said.

"Do you want me to sit here with you?"

"No, it's better for me to be alone. I want him to worry about only one human being at a time."

Henry returned to the fire. He turned off the lantern and built up the fire. Octavius might have slept somewhere close by, slept lightly in the skiff with a pistol in his hand. Octavius had accomplished this feat, a mythical voyage, and now Robert, like some poet to warriors, was going to tell it as they sat around sandbar campfires. He sat and dozed by the fire. He imagined himself as Octavius, alone on the river at night, rowing the skiff toward the Gulf and freedom. How Octavius must have felt the enormity of that darkness. Then he thought of nothing at all and listened to the birds calling, a thick rich sound.

He remained by the fire until it burned down. Paul, who had not spoken, sat cross-legged before Hoffman. It struck Henry that Paul was like a worshipper at the feet of an idol. From time to time he offered Hoffman turtle meat or prodded him awake with the switch, but the bird's only response was to hiss and snap his beak.

When Henry finally went to his tent to sleep, he did not say goodnight to Paul. And Paul did not acknowledge his leaving. Paul sat motionless before Hoffman, the switch in one hand and a piece of turtle meat in the other. Now the flies had found the meat and were lighting on Paul, who felt no inclination to brush them away. Paul concentrated hard, trying to focus all his attention of Hoffman. Somehow the bird would *know* he had no choice but to give in to his will.

As Henry lay down to sleep, he felt such a sense of sadness for Octavius that it brought tears to his eyes. He lay on his back and looked up through the mosquito netting at the stars. The birds had stopped calling and there was only the persistent, incessant hum of the insects. He considered going out and telling Paul about his sadness but decided against it. Then the birds began to call again and like Octavius he counted the calls. Before he reached a hundred he was asleep.

Chapter Five

PAUL SAT ON the sand before the bird. He felt mosquitoes swoop close to his face, kept at bay by the insect repellent. The smoke from the small fire he had started drifted over him. Although the smoke stung his eyes, he was willing to endure that because it helped keep the mosquitoes away. It had been hours since Hoffman had tried to put his head under his wing. He looked into the bird's dark eyes that reflected the glow from the fire. The light shined off the bird's red head. He imagined Hoffman sailing high above the river, looking down at the tops of the trees, at the meandering loops the brown river made across the flat land, at the white sandbars.

"What's it like looking at dead things?"

He felt uncomfortable in the bird's gaze. Hoffman did not acknowledge the sound of his voice.

"I couldn't see what you see." Paul imagined himself sailing above the river in a hang glider, the only way he could think of that would allow him to experience flight as Hoffman did. He might see a dead deer on a sandbar but not a rabbit. Hoffman would see it all, every creature that had been dragged down to death.

He offered the bird a piece of meat, but Hoffman hissed at him. Paul began to feel sleepy. All the coffee he had drunk seemed to be having no effect. He stood up and walked back and forth in front of the bird. Hoffman did not move; he kept his eyes fixed on him.

Paul stopped his pacing and picked up a piece of meat. He walked slowly up to the bird until he was an arm's length away. Hoffman did not draw himself up to his full height, but instead turned his head to one side to look at Paul.

"I want you to live."

Hoffman raised himself to his full height. He spread his good wing. For a moment Paul was afraid that he was going to try to fly off his perch and further injure himself.

"Live and fly," Paul cooed, as if he were speaking to a baby. "Live and fly."

Hoffman lowered his wing and again cocked his head to one side to look at Paul.

Paul took a step toward Hoffman, but the bird did not move. He stretched out his hand, holding the meat in his other hand by his side. Hoffman still did not move. Paul moved his hand closer and closer to the vulture's head. He was not sure what he intended to do. Hoffman opened his beak slightly and then closed it. Paul stretched out his index finger and touched Hoffman's beak. He left his finger there for a moment on the smooth surface.

"Live and fly," Paul whispered. "Live and fly."

Then he stepped back, remaining within an arm's reach of the vulture. He held out the piece of meat in his left hand. Hoffman cocked his head to one side and looked at the food with one eye, but then he turned his head away and gazed off into the darkness.

For a few minutes Paul remained standing there, holding out the meat to the bird. Then Paul sat down and reclined on the sand in front of the bird, supporting his head with one arm. Hoffman turned his head back and looked at him. Paul thought of the feel of Hoffman's beak beneath his finger, how smooth it was, like a piece of polished yellow stone.

Paul scooped up a pile of sand to make a pillow and lay his head down on it. Hoffman was no longer looking at him, again turning his head toward the darkness. Then Paul drifted off to sleep. He woke with a start, roused by a swarm of mosquitoes. The fire had burned down to red coals and little smoke was coming off it. Instead of sleeping, Hoffman was looking at him. The bird cocked his head to one side and stretched out his good wing. Paul sat up and applied more mosquito repellent. He hoped that Hoffman had not also slept. He built up the fire and soon smoke was swirling over them again.

He offered Hoffman a piece of meat. The bird carefully and fastidiously took it. He swallowed it. Paul gave him another and another until all the meat was gone. Then Hoffman stuck his head under his wing. Paul sat down on the sand before the bird, thinking of the day Hoffman would fly again, his big but delicate body borne higher and higher on a thermal until he was just a speck in the blue sky. He felt like shouting and waking his companions. They could all have a drink of whiskey to celebrate. But he decided he would let them sleep. He would enjoy a solitary celebration. He went up to the tarp and poured himself a drink of whiskey. Then he returned with the tin cup to sit before Hoffman. He drank the warm whiskey slowly and carefully. When the cup was empty he considered going back to the tent to sleep and taking Hoffman with him but decided to stay with the bird. He lay down on the sand and closed his eyes.

WHEN ROBERT STEPPED out of the tent at sunrise, Paul was asleep before Hoffman. The bird watched with his dark eyes as Robert walked toward them. Paul woke, awakened by the squeak of the sand under Robert's feet.

"He ate!" Paul said. "He ate all the meat. He's going to live."

The others woke. They broke camp and ran a few miles downriver. Paul and Mason went ashore at the first irrigated field they came upon and returned with watermelons and cantaloupes. They stopped on a sandbar and ate them.

Mason walked over to Hoffman and offered him a piece of cantaloupe. Hoffman hissed, flapping his good wing, and clacked his beak.

Henry looked at the glossy shine of Hoffman's dark brown

feathers. "Maybe he could take off your finger. Maybe the book's wrong about that. That beak does look dangerous."

"He's gonna get Paul's finger, not mine," Mason said.

Mason popped the piece of melon into his own mouth. "I guess I'd be proud to be something that don't pay no mind to anything except what's dead or what's getting ready to die. Sails around and waits."

"Vultures clean up carrion," Henry said. "They raise families. They continue themselves. They have a purpose. What's your purpose, Mason?"

"Tennis, women, and whiskey," Mason said. "Sometimes the order changes."

Henry turned to Paul. "And yours?"

"Elizabeth, books, the kids I teach."

"Robert?"

Robert suddenly thought of Elaine, how he had put her at the center of his life just as Paul did Elizabeth. Perhaps before the trip was over he would tell his friends about what had happened in Africa.

"This manuscript."

"All of you are wrong," said Henry.

"It don't appear to me that you're any happier than the rest of us," Mason said.

"It's not a matter of happiness," Henry said. "It's a matter of duty. Responsibility. To have children. To raise them well."

"It's not our fault that you've gotten bored with that grass you study," Paul said.

"You're right," Henry said. "I am bored with that. I thought this trip would clear my head. And it has. I'm beginning to understand what's important in a person's life."

"It's different for everyone," Mason said.

Henry slowly shook his head. "No it's the same."

"Like gravity?" Robert asked.

"Yes, like that," Henry said. "That's a good way of putting it."

Henry took a fine seine and waded out into the river to sample the water off the sandbar. Familiar creatures showed up in the seine: minnows, crayfish, freshwater shrimp. A drop of water seen under the microscope would reveal another invisible world. He wondered what sort of world was going to be revealed in the untranslated portion of Octavius' narrative. It seemed to him that Paul was right. There was not much hope for Octavius. He was like a bit of flotsam borne down the river by a spring flood. Henry was anxious to see if Octavius was satisifed when he returned and had the house and land in his grasp. But then it was taken away by disease. He was going to lose it anyway and probably his life along with it when the Federal troops were pulled out of the South. He dipped the seine in the river a final time. This time it came up empty, not a single living creature caught in the mesh.

THEY WENT DOWN the river. Most of the way they were able to use the motors and by late morning they reached the Georgetown bridge. They lingered, the motors at idle, in the strip of shade cast by the bridge. Two boys, one white and one black, were fishing from the bank.

"What'cha doing with that buzzard?" the older boy asked.

"Fattening him up to eat," Mason said.

"You can't eat a buzzard," the younger boy said.

The older boy gave the younger one a poke in the ribs. Then the younger one understood that Mason was having fun with him.

"I ate a buzzard once," the younger boy said.

They all ignored him.

"Where yawl headed?" the older boy asked.

"Haiti," Paul said.

The older boy stood up, a little angry that the men were still teasing him. "Yawl ain't going to no Haiti."

"No, we ain't going there," Mason said. "We're going to Cuba."

The boy laughed. "The sharks are gonna eat yawl."

"They got beer in Georgetown?" Mason asked.

"Cold beer at my uncle's store," the younger boy said. "You go on up there and get yourself one."

"We're not drinking beer," Henry said. "We're drinking nothing but whiskey and river water."

"Yawl are crazy then," the older boy said.

Mason gave the boys a ten-dollar bill and sent them after a cold six-pack. Then he studied his map. "There's nothing between here and Monticello. Only one railroad bridge. This'll be our last chance."

Soon the boys returned with the beer. Mason gave them each a dollar. Everyone opened a beer. Mason threw his head back and drained his can in one long swallow. Then he opened another one. "Yawl better drink up or I'm getting the last one."

"Go ahead," Paul said. "You deserve it."

They said goodbye to the boys and pointed the boats down river.

Robert sat under the canopy and worked on the next chapter of the narrative. From time to time one of the men asked him questions about it. Mason was particularly persistent. But Robert refused to discuss what he had translated.

Then they stopped for lunch and Paul gutted the fish he had caught and wrapped them in clay from a deposit he found on the bank. He fed the entrails to Hoffman, who eagerly ate them. They lay about under the tarp until the fire had burned down to coals. Then Paul laid the fish in their mud cocoons on the coals along with the rest of the corn, which he had treated in a similar manner.

After the mud had hardened in the fire, they broke the shells open and ate the fish and corn.

"I might get tired of fish in a few days," Mason said.

"Maybe we'll gig some frogs tonight," Henry said.

"You ever eaten a frog?"

"Plenty of times."

"Same as a snake."

"I know something you'll all like, poke salad. Everyone keep a lookout for that."

The men slept under the tarp, but Robert did not feel like sleeping. He wanted to return to the narrative. Off to the west some big thunderheads were building. He wished it would rain so traveling would be cooler.

But it did not rain. The clouds moved off to the northeast. They broke camp and were on the river again.

The same scenery passed by Robert's eyes over and over: sandbars, cypress swamps, stands of gum and tupelo and live oak, and on the high ground, stretches of pines. Sometimes there was pastureland. Once they came upon cattle in the river.

They stopped at another irrigated field. A flexible pipe snaked down to the water, running across a sandbar, and up the bank. They heard the clatter of the pump.

Robert and Mason, each carrying a canvas sack, went to steal vegetables. They walked up through the trees, moving slowly and cautiously because of the danger of snakes, to the edge of an open field. Already they knew that corn was there. Stalks were up in the trees where raccoons had carried them after they had raided the field.

They left the tree line and entered the corn, which was higher than their heads. They heard the hiss of the big sprinkler that threw water in a three-hundred foot circle, but they could not see it.

"Let's find the road," Mason said. "They'd plant tomatoes and such next to it. Drive right up to do the harvesting."

They walked within the arc of the sprinkler. Water dripped from the corn leaves, which glistened in the sunlight. Mud sucked at their sandals. As the sprinkler passed over them, the cold water felt good on their faces. Then it was gone and they were outside the arc, walking on the dry ground again.

The field ended. They crossed a dirt track, the charcoal-grey dust as fine as talcum power. The track ran along one side of the rectangular field, bordered by pines on one side and hardwoods on the others.

"You go back down toward the river," Mason said. "I'll walk up the road. I wish I'd find some pole beans. It seems like somebody on this river would be growing pole beans."

Robert walked along the track. A pattern of tractor tires was imprinted in the dust. The track bent around the side nearest the river. He came upon a garden. A tractor was parked on the other side of the road. There were tomatoes and cantaloupes and huge squash plants, the big yellow fruit hanging pendulous from the stems.

He thought of yelling for Mason but decided against it. Someone might be around and there was no use letting anyone know that they were there. He began to fill his bag.

"Tomatoes are high this year," a woman's voice said.

He turned to see a middle-aged woman standing by the tractor. She wore jeans and a straw cowboy hat. She held a revolver in her hand that she had taken from the holster on her belt. It was no ladies' gun. He supposed it was a .44. Her face was sunburned and creased. She looked like she knew how to use the big pistol.

"Been a dry summer," she said. "Pumping that water ain't free."

"You don't need that," he said. "I can pay."

Then he realized that he was wearing only a pair of swimming trunks and river sandals. His billfold was at the boat.

"Five dollars a tomato," she said. "Cantaloupes and squash are the same."

"Look—" he began.

"I should just shoot your damn eyes out," she said.

Mason came around the side of the tractor, walking quietly on the fine dust of the road. She saw his eyes on Mason and turned, but she was too slow.

"Boo!" Mason said.

He stepped forward and grabbed her gun hand. Then he twisted the gun away from her. She said something Robert could not understand, a sharp sound like the bark of a fox. She came at Mason, who pushed her down hard into the dust. She lay there looking old and confused. Robert hoped she had not broken a bone.

Mason threw the gun toward the trees. It flashed in the sunlight as it crossed the open space between them and the darkness of the trees. It fell, rattling the branches before it landed with a heavy thud in a tangle of briars.

For a moment they all stood looking at each other in a sort of suspension, as if their feet were mired in mud. She struggled to her feet.

"I'll feed you to the gators!" she yelled.

"Run!" Mason shouted.

Robert broke for the corn and ran hard across the rows, the leaves whipping against his face. Mason ran at his shoulder. They were running through the sprinkler, and it was hard going because of the mud. They both fell. Then they were up and running again, this time on dry ground. Finally they reached the trees where they knelt together, breathing hard.

"She coming after us?" Robert asked.

"No," Mason said. "She don't look like a runner to me."

"She's on her truck radio right now calling the sheriff."

Mason shook his head. "She's not calling nobody."

"Why wouldn't she? We just stole from her. You assaulted her."

Mason lay on the ground, his white clothes covered with grey mud, and laughed. For a time it seemed to Robert as if he were never going to stop laughing. Mason was not going to tell Robert that what he found so funny was that he had just engaged in petty theft with a university professor,

"Come on, Mason," Robert said. "We've got to go. She's calling the sheriff."

Mason stood up. "She's not calling nobody. That lady has got some fine looking marijuana plants set out in the corn up at the other end of the field. The sheriff won't be coming out here."

Mason picked up his sack and began to examine the contents. "She grows some mighty good looking squash.But no pole beans."

"You could have gotten me shot," said Robert.

"Maybe you're right. She might have shot us both, to protect her crop. Folks kill other folks over a lot less. Yes, sir, she'd have shot us and we'd have ended up in a shallow grave in her vegetable garden. She'd grow some mighty big cantaloupes out of us. Win first prize at the county fair."

Mason pulled Robert to his feet. Robert took the canvas sack.

As they walked carefully through the trees, Robert was grateful no one had been hurt. The woman was probably still looking for her gun in the tangle of grapevines and briars. She would cut a stick for snakes before she went after it.

They reached the boat where they quickly loaded themselves and the produce and moved off downriver. Luckily this was a section of the river deep enough for the motors, and in a few minutes they were far away from the field. There would be no way for the woman to follow except by water.

Mason told the story to the others, shouting it over the sound of the motors, as the boats traveled side by side on parallel tracks, heading south toward the sea.

Chapter Six

THEY TRAVELED ALL afternoon and into the evening but saw no more irrigated fields or even pastures. The river was lined with trees, the land cut periodically by creeks. Sometimes they were able to use the motors, but at other times they had to pole the boats, and once found it necessary to get out and tow them. When they were under power, Robert sat beneath the canopy and worked on the manuscript. He was becoming accustomed to Octavius' hand.

When the sun started to drop below the trees, they began to see deer, come down to the river to drink. The deer were all does, often with spotted fawns beside them. They stood and watched the boats approach for a few moments before they gracefully bounded across a sandbar, white tails flashing, and disappeared into the green wall of the trees.

"That's what I want to eat tonight," Henry said.

"Just don't shoot one with a fawn," Paul cautioned.

Robert removed the Mannlicher from its case and took up a position in the bow of the boat. Henry poled the boat, most of the time simply letting it drift with the current. Everyone sat still and did not talk. It was getting close to dark. Bats twisted overhead. Whippoorwills began to call from the timber on the bluff side of the river. The chorus of insects increased in volume, new clicks and hums coming into play as it grew darker.

The river made a loop to the right. As they came around the

bend, where there was a big sandbar on the long inside curve, Robert saw three does standing at the river's edge. They turned their heads toward the boats. They stood in the half light, looking insubstantial, as if they were projections upon a darkened screen and not real animals at all whose hearts were beating at this instant, pumping blood for flight through their lungs. He brought up the rifle and put the telescopic sight on the larger doe. She was sniffing the air, trying to identify the cloud of effluvium: man-scent and oil and gas, whose outer edges had reached her. The others turned toward the trees, on the edge of flight, but she hesitated. He shot her through the shoulder. She collapsed instantly on the sand. He guessed the bullet had passed through both the heart and lungs.

After they hung the deer from a tripod made of hickory poles, Henry butchered her in the light from gasoline lanterns. Soon flies swarmed about the carcass. Fat hairy moths circled the lanterns. Henry cut steaks off a haunch for their dinner. Paul fed meat to Hoffman.

Paul constructed a frame of willow branches. They cut the rest of the meat into strips and began to smoke it over a slow fire. The smoke, rich with the scent of the meat, drifted back and forth over the sandbar and stung the men's eyes.

They made another fire upwind from the curing meat and cooked the steaks and the squash. They were all hungry, and they easily ate the entire haunch and half of the other one. Then they lay around the fire and drank warm whiskey while the moths circled around the lanterns and night birds called from the trees. The moon rode low over the tops of cypresses and outlined the tops against the night sky.

"We want to hear," Paul said.

Robert removed his translation from the waterproof bag and began to read.

I Confound My Pursuers
I woke to the sounds of the birds. For a moment I lay listening to those beautiful calls, an

*instant of peace and repose that was shattered
when I remembered what I had done. I looked
up at the green canopy of willows, shot through
with golden light, arching over my head, and
cried for myself and for the man whom I had
loved and killed. I cried until my cheeks were
wet with tears and I tasted the salt from them.*

*After I ate a few slices of venison and drank
some water, I felt better. As I lay in the creek, I
heard no human sound and saw no one pass on
the river. There was no reason why anyone
should have discovered my dead master. I
planned to remain in the creek until dusk. But
late in the afternoon the mosquitoes, which hung
in clouds about me, finally drove me out of it
and into the open air of the river, which was free
of insects.*

*I was approaching a bend in the river when
I heard a rifle shot. I took the skiff in close to
the bank. I sat there for some time, hardly dar-
ing to breathe, a rifle in my hands. But I heard
no other sounds. The shot seemed to come from
the river and not from the trees.*

*I took the rifle, both pistols, and a Bowie
knife and left the boat. I worked my way along
the bank to a place where I could see a sandbar
through the willows. I crawled across the sand
like a snake until I had a clear view of the sandbar.*

*Two young men, one white and one a man of
color, were skinning a bear. Their pirogue was
drawn up on the sand. The man of color wore
homespun; the white man's clothes were deerskin. I supposed the man of color was a freed
slave. No hunter could afford to own a slave. I*

*knew that if they found me they would abandon
the bear. I was worth more money than either of
them would likely see for the rest of their lives.*

*I crawled closer, following a line of low wil-
low bushes, my journey made less difficult because they were so engaged with their work. They
began to shift the position of the carcass. The
bear was of great size and both of them had their
shoulders against the carcass, laughing to each
other as it resisted their efforts to roll it over.*

*I brought up the rifle on the white man and
shot him through the side as he pushed against
the carcass with his arms outstretched, hoping
the ball would pass through his heart or lungs.
As the white man dropped to the sand, I rose to
my feet and drawing the pistols from my belt ran
across the sand.*

*As the man of color turned to look at me, I
heard the sound of my own breathing and the
sand squeaking beneath my feet, and it seemed
that I was going to be running forever toward
him. He half-ran and half-crawled across the
sand, going for his rifle, which lay propped
against a willow. I was close now, and I stopped
to fire a pistol. It misfired. I dropped it and
shifted the other one to my right hand. I shot
him as he turned toward me, the ball entering
his bare chest just above his navel. A red flower
blossomed there.*

*He reached for the wound with one hand and
tried to bring up the rifle with the other. I pulled
my Bowie knife and closing the distance between
us plunged it into his heart. He fell back on the
sand and died.*

I dragged him to the carcass of the bear. I

removed his clothes and then mine and dressed him in my fine linen garments, the cast-off clothes of my master. I put my Bowie knife in his hand. I hoped no one would find him until the vultures had eaten their fill (they would go for the eyes and the soft flesh of the cheeks first and soon he would be unrecognizable), and my pursuers would suppose that I had shot the bear and then the wounded animal had killed me. I lay my rifle beside the pair and took up their rifles, both fine arms. Strode Maury's rifle had his initials embossed in silver on the stock. If I were lucky, the search for me would end here on this sand-bar.

I brought the skiff down to the bar. Then I examined the contents of the pirogue. There was powder and lead and bullet molds and a supply of patches. And salt and an iron cooking pot. There were also fishing hooks and lines. I had forgotten these when I left the cabin. There were the raw skins of two bears.

I took the sextant and chronometer from the skiff and the Bowditch along with the charts. I took the ax and the sharpening stone. I took the remainder of the venison and the shotgun. But I left the two rifles and the bullet molds and all the lead and powder.

I loaded the white man's body into the pirogue. By now it was dusk, and I was thankful for the coming night. I had stripped him of his deerskin clothes, intending to wear either those or the man of color's homespun, but the deer-skins were greasy and fouled with excrement and blood. The homespun trousers were in the same state. I washed the trousers in the river and put them in the pirogue. For the present I would go naked. I wore only the man of color's leather belt to provide a place for the hunter's Bowie in its sheath and my pistols. Later I would dispose of the deerskins.

After going downriver a few miles I was confronted with how to dispose of the white man. I would like to have weighted his body with rocks and sunk it in some deep pool, but there was nothing larger than a pebble on the river. So I buried the clothes on a sandbar where the digging was easy and then cut the white man into parts and every mile or so threw one into the river. The turtles would eat the flesh. Soon there would be nothing left but his bones, lying white and clean on the sand. I threw the bear skins into the river, for they were beginning to stink.

I washed the filth from myself and the pirogue and then plastered myself with mud against the mosquitoes. I turned the pirogue into the river and paddled hard with the pine paddle for a long time until, exhausted, I let the boat drift in the gentle current, the air about me warm as blood and the stars shining overhead.

"PAUL, YOU RECKON old Hoffman's great-great-granddaddy had a few good meals off them folks Octavius killed?" Mason asked. "Looks like Octavius knew something about vultures. Yawl could have had a club. See whose pet vulture smelled the baddest."

Paul did not reply.

"Those birds probably still tell stories about it. There was the bear too. I forgot about that. It was like Christmas and Thanksgiving at the same time for them."

"Leave it be, Mason," Robert said.

Mason wished he could have lived at the time. There was plenty of land, and all a man had to do to get it was take it. Now somebody owned it all. Even the trailer where he lived and the land it rested on belonged to somebody else.

Paul got up and went to tend the smoking fire. As he worked on it, the smoke drifted over them, bringing again the rich scent of the meat. Paul called for Henry to come look at the meat and Henry went. They began to discuss how long it would take to drive all the water out of it. But then their talk turned to Octavius.

"In the space of two days, he's killed three people," Paul said. "After he did it he must have been the loneliest man in Mississippi."

"I suppose he was," Henry said.

"We know what he did. We know about approximately where he must have been on the river. But we really don't know that much about him."

Henry considered how Octavius was an educated man, better educated than many of his students. He was at home in two languages. But Octavius was still just delivering the facts, hiding whatever was going on inside him, the intoxication with freedom and the disgust he surely must have felt at what he was being forced to do.

He was leaving out of the narrative a description of the wild stream of emotions that must have been coursing through his mind.

"I don't think we're going to find out that much."

"Maybe later he'll start thinking about what's happened to him."

"Perhaps. But maybe all he's thinking about is Haiti and getting himself out of Mississippi."

Paul was wondering how the story of Octavius was affecting Henry. He wanted to ask him how the narrative was playing to a man whose ancestors had been slaves on the plantation Octavius finally owned. It was possible that some had remained and worked for Octavius.

They heard Mason laugh. Hoffman, silhouetted between them and the fire, puffed up his feathers and hissed.

"Don't let Mason get at you," Henry said.

"I won't," Paul said.

"Has Mason ever said anything about me?"

"Only that you're a good player."

Henry wondered if Paul would have revealed any racial slurs on the part of Mason. He decided he probably would not. So he would never know for sure about Mason.

"I wish we'd left him at home," Paul said. "He's angry at the whole world."

"We're stuck with him," said Henry.

Then they left off talking of Mason or Octavius and concentrated on tending the fire and the meat.

Mason and Robert sat before the fire. Robert considered how they were geographically covering the same ground as Octavius, but thankfully were in another time, the trail cooled to absolute zero, the arenas where Octavius fought vanished forever. He wondered if he could find the foundations of the cabin, digging down through the sandy loam to discover the dark circles of postholes or the remains of the chimney or hearth.

"I'd liked to have been on the river then," Mason said. "Met Octavius."

"Octavius would've killed both of us," Robert said.

"You think so?"

"I think Hoffman's ancestors would have picked our bones. I think we'd have been no problem for Octavius at all."

Mason got up and tossed another log on the dying fire. He imagined standing guard outside the circle of light while his companions slept. No one, not even a man like Octavius would be able to locate him if he remained motionless. Once, while hunting for deer in a dry creek bed, Mason had sat perfectly still for so long that a cock quail had walked up between his outstretched legs.

Paul and Henry walked up.

"Robert, I'll pole the boat tomorrow," Henry said. "I want you working on the rest of that translation. I want to find out what he does."

The others agreed.

Henry wished he had the language so he could do the translation and by doing that come in more direct contact with Octavius. He was sure to be able to understand Octavius in ways that were beyond the reach of Robert.

"We'll make the camps," Mason said. "We'll do the cooking. All you got to do is put that thing into English."

Robert pointed out that it was difficult work. He thought he could do a chapter a day, not much more.

He felt tired and went to sleep before the others, who seemed not inclined at all to sleep. As he lay in his tent he heard Paul and Henry talking as they adjusted the fire under the meat.

Robert considered getting up and working on the translation. Instead he closed his eyes and drifted off to sleep, the smell of the curing meat filling the tent.

Chapter Seven

ROBERT WOKE IN the morning to a humming sound unlike the familiar buzz of the insects. He crawled out of his tent and discovered that he had been the last to awaken.

Paul and Henry were removing the cured meat from the willow frame. Everywhere there were flies, the source of the sound, flies swarming through the smoke above the frame and flies, a tight knot of them, about the remains of the deer. Mason was sitting in one of the boats beneath the canopy, cradling a shotgun in his arms.

As Robert pulled his sleeping pad out of the tent, the shotgun went off. He turned just in time to see a large black bird falling toward the river where it hit with a splash and lay crippled, beating a single unbroken wing against the water. It was a vulture.

"Stop shooting the birds!" Paul shouted.

Three more vultures were flapping desperately to climb over a low stand of willows at the down stream end of the sandbar. Mason shot at them too, loosening a few feathers, but then the birds cleared the trees and were gone.

Hoffman watched them from his perch. He flapped his good wing. Mason shoved shells, the brass ends gleaming in the sunlight, into the magazine of the shotgun. He shot the downed bird again, the pattern of shot tearing the water around it. Then the bird was still. It floated past Mason and down stream.

"I ought to make you eat that bird," Paul said.

"You won't make a pet out of that one," Mason said. "We could feed it to Hoffman. Do you think buzzards are particular about eating their own kind?"

"You didn't have to do that."

"We're shooting deer out of season. And a doe at that. We're stealing from farmers. What difference does it make if I want to shoot a buzzard? It's against the law to do that too."

Henry left the smoking rack and walked across the sand to the river's edge. "Because it's killing without a reason."

"Those birds are the ugliest thing God has created," Mason said.

"Don't shoot another one," said Paul.

"Do you love buzzards, Henry?" Mason asked. "I know Paul does. I don't."

Paul started for Mason.

"Wait," Robert called after him.

Robert ran across the sand, reaching Paul just as he was starting to step into the boat. He wrapped his arms around him and pulled him away. Paul continued to struggle against him, but Robert held on tight. Gradually Paul's struggles subsided. Mason, in contempt, had turned his back to them.

"I'm all right," Paul said. "I'm all right."

Robert released him. "No use fighting over a dead vulture. We've got a long way to go. We've got to get along."

Paul said nothing. He walked to the down stream end of the sandbar. For a moment Robert thought he was going to go into the river after the vulture, but he did not. He sat on the sand, his back to them.

Paul was thinking about getting off the river the next time he had a chance. He could care for Hoffman at home until the bird's wing healed. He and Elizabeth would watch Hoffman awkwardly launch himself off the deck of their house and flap his wings until he gained altitude. Then with fixed wings he would soar above the trees, climbing higher and higher until he disappeared from view.

"He's still looking at us," he would say to Elizabeth. "He's the eyes of God." And Elizabeth would understand. She would put her arms around him and they would gaze up into the vacant sky where Hoffman still soared, buoyed by the thermals.

Later, as they made preparations to leave, Paul avoided Mason, refusing to speak to him. Robert suggested that they change partners, but Paul refused.

"I can stand that son of a bitch," Paul said. "He's like the heat. He won't bother me if I don't think about him too much."

They pushed the boats out into the river and left the sandbar and the remains of the deer to the vultures. Paul and Henry had wrapped the smoked meat in packets of cheesecloth, which now hung from the canopies of the boats. The rich smell surrounded them as they moved off down the river.

They ate the remainder of the cantaloupes for breakfast, slicing them with their knives and filling their mouths, afterwards trailing their hands in the river to cleanse them of the sticky juice. They saw no more farmers' fields to raid. The river banks unfolded as a combination of oak and pine-covered bluffs or cypress and gum swamps. Now there was Spanish bayonet growing beneath the trees and thick stands of evergreen laurel. The color of the river had changed from a loam brown to that of weak coffee.

It had grown unusually hot, so hot that the wind created by the movement of the boats was no relief. Far down the river was a wall of white clouds, whose tops were swelling upward into the perfectly blue sky.

No turtles sunned themselves on riverside logs, which all had a bleached cast from the action of the river and the sun. No kingfishers flashed blue and white, flying in their jerky manner across the river. No schools of minnows flashed silver in the shallows. No hawks hung in the air, turning in slow circles over river and forest. And with the departure of the animals the insects had increased in numbers. The boats moved through swarms of dragonflies. The water in places was littered with the dying hatch of some sort of insect. Henry scooped them up with a net and studied them with his magnifying glass, searching his books for their identity. Mason kept asking him what they were. Henry told him their scientific name but refused to reveal their common one. Although Mason kept at him, Henry just shook his head. Robert returned to the translation. Now they cruised under power.

When they stopped to switch fuel tanks on the motors, Mason and Paul started in on each other again.

"You'd kill every living thing on this river if you had a chance," Paul said.

"You gonna report me to the game warden?" Mason asked.

"I don't care about that."

"Well, what do you mean?"

"It upsets the balance of things."

Paul spoke softly. Robert could tell that he was serious.

"How?"

"Those birds watch death. Like God."

"The turtles right now are eating that bird I killed," Mason said. "They're doing the watching."

"We won't see any game today. You wait and see. You killed that bird. That's why."

"You should stop reading those books. Filling your head full of crazy ideas."

Henry explained how animals took refuge from the intolerable heat. They found a shady place and were still.

"All the animals except us," Robert said. "Not so smart of us."

"There's nothing in this world besides what we can see," Henry said. "No magic. Mason could shoot a hundred vultures. He could shoot a thousand. And it wouldn't change a thing."

"Don't you worry," Mason said. "You boys come up empty handed and I'll take care of lunch."

Once they were underway again Robert returned to the translation.

The boats swung slowly around a bend (they were poling now) and there was a line of jugs marking a cat fisherman's lines. Mason poled the boat toward them.

Paul shook his head. "You can't do that."

Mason said something Robert and Henry could not make it out. Paul made a reply and put down his pole. Mason pointed to the jugs. Paul shook his head.

While Paul sat with his arms folded, Mason used a paddle to scull the boat along the line of jugs. Robert had poled the boat into a patch of shade next to the bank where he and Henry sat and drank some warm water and watched.

Robert realized that Mason was not looking for fish. He was removing the six inch-long lead bars the fisherman used to anchor the jugs. He only took five of them, leaving the jugs to drift away downstream.

As they moved down river again, Robert brought their boat in close to Mason's.

"What are you going to do with that lead?" Henry asked.

"What's the scientific name for lead?" Mason asked.

"Lead is lead. You gonna set out some lines tonight?'

"Maybe."

Henry asked him more questions, but Mason was evasive.

At noon they halted on a sandbar. They put up the tarp near the water's edge, as far as possible from the thick tangle of vines and laurel and cane where mosquitoes sought the shade.

Robert worked on the translation and watched Paul fishing for catfish at a pool at the head of the sandbar. He had saved in a plastic bag some of the deer's inner organs for this purpose. They stank properly, but he was having no luck.

Henry was making a drawing of an insect. He sat cross-legged with the drawing pad across his knees, his identification guides spread out before him. Mason was asleep.

Robert began to study the first sentence of the new section of translation. He found it difficult to concentrate in the heat. Sweat dripped from his face onto the legal pad. He watched Paul casting his bait out into the pool, the entrails flashing in the sunlight. The bait hit the dark water with a splash. Paul raised and lowered the rod tip as he worked it across the bottom. It took him perhaps five minutes to complete the process. He moved a little farther upstream and started over again. Robert counted the people Octavius had killed and then counted them again. Then the murderous deeds of the Duke in *The White Book* passed through his mind. Jealousy had driven the Duke to kill just as it had Octavius. But at least Octavius' deed had been one when he was unexpectedly caught in a violent passion.

The Duke had carefully planned his revenge. He wondered if later in the manuscript, perhaps in this section, Octavius would decide not to kill. Perhaps he was already done with killing.

Henry returned his books and the sketch pad to a waterproof bag. He walked down to the water and boarded one of the boats. He pushed it out into the river and started the motor.

Robert stood up and yelled to him. Henry smiled and waved. Then he was gone downriver, soon out of sight around a bend. Mason was still asleep. Paul concentrated on his fishing. He had just turned his head briefly when Henry left and then had returned to working his bait across the bottom.

The sound of the motor was fading into the distance. Abruptly it stopped. Henry had not gone far. Robert returned to working on the translation. Somewhere from deep within the trees a bird called furiously. Then it was silent.

Soon the motor started again, first at an idle and then at full throttle, the sound approaching nearer and nearer until Henry came into view. After he beached the boat, he bent over to gather up something from the bottom. Paul turned to watch him too.

When Henry straightened up, his arms were full of pokeweed. He was smiling as he walked across the sand toward Robert.

"We'll have the rest of the corn and poke salad," he said. "We don't need meat."

Mason woke up and admired the poke weed. "Nice. But I ain't a damn vegetarian. I want meat."

Paul gave up on fishing and returned to the shade of the tarp. He checked to make sure that Hoffman had fresh water. Then he drank some water himself and stretched out to sleep.

"They won't be biting until it cools off," Henry said.

"Think so?" Mason asked.

"If there're any fish at all."

Mason rose and picked up his daypack, which sagged from the weight of the lead bars. "Oh, I expect there're some fat catfish laying on the bottom where it's cool." He started toward the river.

"Don't you need a pole?"

Mason ignored Henry and kept walking, the sunlight brilliant on his white clothes. He sat on the sand by the edge of the deep pool where Paul had been fishing, the pack between his legs. He took one of the lead bars out of the pack and hefted it. Then he turned his back toward them and removed something from the pack.

Paul woke up. "What's he doing?"

Paul stood up but remained under the shade of the tarp. "Who knows," Henry said.

Henry was trying to sleep and did not bother to raise his head to look. Mason tossed something into the pool. It made a solid sound when it hit. Mason stood looking at the water. Then the water erupted from the pool, the spray rising over Mason, the sound of the explosion reaching them an instant later. Robert dropped his work, papers scattering before him. "That damn fool's fishing with dynamite!"

Mason was laughing as he spread his arms wide. Behind him fish, killed by the explosion, rose to litter the surface of the pool, their bellies white against the dark water.

"Come on! Mason shouted. "You want to eat! They're right here."

JAKE

PAIGE

Chapter Eight

THEY ATE ONLY a few of the fish Mason killed, mostly catfish and some bream. There were a few gars shaped like torpedoes, their long snouts full of teeth. These they discarded. They filled the live well with the others. Mason was pleased with himself. He had four sticks of dynamite left.

"Remember them loaves and fishes in the Bible," Mason said. "Why, I'm just like Jesus. With this dynamite I'll feed the multitude."

Mason slit open a gar and removed the inner organs. He walked over to where Hoffman was sitting on his perch and held out the entrails to the bird. Hoffman flapped his good wing and hissed.

"Ah, you're a pretty one." Mason turned to Paul. "See, I'm sweet-talking your buzzard."

"I think he doesn't love you," Henry said.

Mason turned back to Hoffman. "You love me don't you. You wouldn't want to eat my finger."

"I believe he would," Paul said.

Mason stepped closer to Hoffman and held out the entrails.

"Be careful," Robert said.

Mason put the entrails closer to Hoffman's beak. The bird snapped at him, and Mason jumped backwards, falling down on the sand. Hoffman hopped off his perch, picked up the entrails, and ate them. Mason sat on the sand, examining his hand.

"Did he get you?" Henry asked.

"No, I'm too quick for him," said Mason.

"Vultures are patient," Paul said. "He'll wait."

A biting fly appeared on the sandbar. They applied more insect repellent. Paul complained the most about both the heat and the insects. He left them and poled a boat across to the bluff side of the river.

Robert swatted at a fly. "Just as many bugs over there."

"Hey, are they biting?" Mason yelled.

Paul nodded his head in affirmation. Then Mason asked him what he was doing. Paul ignored him. He was out of the boat, poking a stick into the face of the bluff.

"Birds sometimes build nests in holes," Henry said. "Maybe he's looking for eggs."

Then Paul stepped out of his swimming trunks. He pulled a handful of clay out of the face of the bluff. He brought it to the water's edge and wet it. Then he began to smear the clay on his body.

Paul returned to the sandbar, his body covered with wet clay. He stood out in the sunlight, his arms spread wide. "See, no more problem with flies." Flies buzzed about him but none settled on him.

"It ain't worth it," Mason said. Henry and Robert agreed.

They loaded the boats and went down the river. Ahead the sky was black with the storm. Thunder rumbled in the distance; the sky was lit with flashes of lightning. Robert expected the storm to blow itself out long before they reached it. Henry calculated, by observing the interval between the lightning flashes and the rumble of the thunder, that the storm was twenty or thirty miles away.

The bluff on the right hand side soon dropped away; the river on both sides was bordered by cypress swamps. The water was too shallow to use the motors. Paul stood in the stern, the mud now baked to a hard shell on his body, and maneuvered the boat through the shallows. Mason lay beneath the canopy, his straw hat pulled down low over his eyes. He appeared to be asleep, but Robert, who was working on the translation, doubted if anyone could sleep in the fierce heat.

The swamp seemed never ending. As far as they could see, there were cypresses. And now the storm appeared to be drifting toward them. No one needed Henry's calculations to know that soon it would be right on top of them. Mason had awakened and was examining his maps, looking for a creek where they could run the boats up into the cypresses.

Mason had always been interested in maps. Once he had stolen a relief globe out of his high school library. Then, after he had done it, the globe hidden under one of his grandmother's quilts in the back of his truck, he realized he had no place to keep it. It was not something he could conceal in his tiny bedroom in the trailer. So he hid it in the woods at the end of a soybean field which began just beyond the strip of grass that bordered the trailer. He hung it in the center of a stand of sweet gum saplings and for the rest of the spring and then into the summer he would walk out and look at it, sometimes tracing the spine of the Himalayas or the course of the Nile. Then one day he found it shattered. Someone had shot it to pieces. The librarian at the school never replaced it.

He knew there were people who made their living making maps, but at the same time he knew he would never be one of them. Yet Henry had grown up just as poor as he had, and now he was a professor at the university. Mason was not exactly sure how Henry had managed to make himself a college professor. Once he had thought it was because Henry was black and had been given money to go to school by the government. But now he was beginning suspect that it was something else, maybe simply Henry's curiosity about the natural world. To Mason one bird singing was the same as any bird. But Henry wanted to know the name of the bird and its habits. Mason found a creek on the map.

Mason folded up the map. "We're two bends away." He picked up a pole and took a position in the bow. Robert did the same.

They reached the creek only minutes before the storm broke. The trees bent in the wind; big drops of rain splattered into the river. The air was cool; the insects had vanished.

As they ran the boats up against the trunk of a big cypress, the boats cutting a path through green patches of duckweed, and tied off the mooring lines to the knees, the storm broke upon them.

Robert looked down the creek and out onto the river. The open water was churned into a froth by the wind and rain; the dark sky was lit by sheets of lightning. The wind howled in the tops of the cypresses; cypress needles and cones fell to litter the coffee-colored water. The rain drummed on the canvas canopy above his head. As he watched, a big cypress came down into the creek with a great splash, partially blocking the channel.

Paul stood in the bow of the boat, his arms raised to the sky. Hoffman sat on his perch under the canopy calmly watching Paul. Mason was yelling at him to get out of the rain; Henry warned him about the lightning. But Paul ignored them. He stood in the driving rain, which soon washed his body clean of its coating of mud. When he finally retreated to the shelter of the canopy, he was shivering.

Mason, laughing, threw him a towel. "Dumb. A human lightning rod." Paul, who was dry now, had his swimming trunks back on and a T-shirt. The rain still was falling hard, but the wind had let up. The storm moved off to the northeast. Once the rain had turned to a gentle drizzle and the sound of the thunder was fading in the distance, they took the boats back onto the river. Robert returned to the translation.

Late in the afternoon they came upon a dead cypress filled with cattle egrets. The birds' white feathers shone in the light from the sun, which was low in the sky behind them.

Hoffman turned his head to one side and looked at the birds.

"Them birds ain't like you," Mason said. "You're like one of them fallen ones down in the pit looking up at the pure angels walking the golden streets of heaven."

Hoffman turned toward the sound of Mason's voice and hissed at him.

"What would happen if you drowned on this river and Hoffman picked your bones?" Paul said. "And you ended up in a heaven of vultures."

"Then I'd know I was in Hell. You keep a sharp watch for snags. This place is full of 'em."

Paul turned his attention back to the river.

The river meandered in soft loops across the flat land, bordered on both sides by the cypress swamp.

"How much more of this swamp?" Robert asked.

Mason looked at his map. "It goes on for three or four grid squares. All this land is real low."

Then it was dusk and still the sides of the river were lined with cypress. They decided to camp for the night on a small mid-river sandbar, barely large enough for the tents.

As they set up the camp, they began to hear alligators grunting from the swamp. They had not seen an alligator yet, although they had talked about their presence from time to time.

"They'll be thick from here to the Gulf," Henry said.

Once it grew dark Mason shined a light onto the low banks, revealing a scattering of red dots, the pairs of dots alligators' eyeshine. But the alligators were shy and remained in the light for only a few seconds. None of them were of any size.

"Just right for barbecued gator tail," Mason said.

He had Henry hold the light and shot one of them with the Mannlicher. He made a good head shot, and the gator died in its tracks. Mason and Henry took a boat and returned with the tail, which Mason barbecued on a stick over the fire, basting it with his cousin's sauce.

"Somebody needs to sit up all night," Robert said. "Too many gators around."

They agreed to a system of watches.

After they ate barbecued gator tail and bread, which Robert baked over the coals in a Dutch oven, along with the rest of the poke salad, they sat under the tarp and listened to Robert read.

Scott Ely

An Unexpected Encounter

I smelled wood smoke on the breeze. As I cautiously worked my way downstream, I heard the sound of an ax on wood. Someone was camped nearby. I decided to run the boat up into a creek and wait for them to sleep. Then I would carefully drift by them. I did not want a repetition of my encounter with the bear hunters.

I remained in the creek for three hours by the chronometer until one o'clock in the morning. The smell of smoke was still on the breeze and the chopping continued. I wondered if someone was building a cabin, but I could not imagine why he would do it at night.

Finally I realized that I would have to scout the camp and learn the disposition of it. I could not risk an encounter unless I knew how many men were there.

I went up through the pines carrying a rifle, the pistols stuck in my belt, and the Bowie knife in its sheath. I followed the sound of the ax. By now I was convinced it was a solitary ax man. It was easy to walk quietly on the thick carpet of needles. The trees were so large they had shaded out the undergrowth.

When I saw the light of a fire, I went down on my belly and carefully worked my way toward the light. I knew that if it were a camp of several men they might have pickets stationed out in the darkness. So every few yards I lay still on the needles and looked into the darkness ahead of me, straining my eyes to see some movement that would reveal a watcher.

The chopping continued. Abruptly it stopped.

I lay stretched out on the needles until it started again. I moved forward and drew close to the circle of light thrown by the fire. It was then that I realized there were two sources of light. I peered around the side of a big pine and saw a large conical mound in the center of a clearing. I realized that I had come upon the camp of a charcoal maker. The mound was a kiln.

The chopping stopped. A man ascended the kiln and threw a log into the open hole in the top. Sparks shot up into the night sky, the light reflecting off the branches of the pines. When he descended the mound and the chopping began again, I turned to go. I felt safe, because I knew such charcoal makers led solitary lives. There was not enough money to be made in the practice for two men.

But when I took the first step, careful to keep the trunk of the pine between me and the camp, a female form darted past me, headed toward the kiln. The woman ran badly with a sort of tottering gait. The man yelled something.

I stepped out from behind the tree. The man stood looking at me but was unable to see because he was blinded by the firelight. He was perfectly outlined. I brought up the rifle and put a bullet into his chest. He dropped cleanly to the ground.

The woman, who I now saw was a woman of color like the man, crossed my line of sight, an ax in her hands, running with that same, awkward gait toward the river.

I ran after her. I went out of the darkness and into the light, past the charcoal kiln and the dead man, and into the darkness again. I thought that perhaps the dead man had been sent here to burn charcoal by some plantation owner. The woman was surely his wife. It was necessary that she die too or she would betray me.

When I saw the lighter darkness of the river ahead of me, I slowed my run to a walk. Then I stopped and reloaded the rifle. Strode Maury and I once had contests doing it in the dark. We would time each other. I was always faster.

Then I ran through the trees, taking a curving path downriver, so that I would be able to intercept her if she had reached a boat and was already on the water and at the same time avoid having her ambush me with the ax.

I reached the bluff. There was no boat. She was in the river, swimming out across a deep pool toward a sandbar on the other side. She held the ax with her free hand and swam with a sidestroke. I went down the face of the bluff, half-running and half-falling, the sand unsteady beneath my feet. Then I was in the water, swimming with the same stroke as she and holding the rifle and powder horn above my head. I kept my eyes on her wet head, which shone in the moonlight.

She disappeared beneath the water for a moment, but then reappeared, swimming with that same steady stroke. She reached the shallows and stumbled to her feet. What she should have done was to try to kill me before I was able to stand, but instead she started toward the sand and fell. I felt the river bottom. I gained my feet. She ran toward the sand, the water splashing about her. I brought up the rifle on her and squeezed the trigger. The hammer came forward, but there was only a click. The powder was wet.

I reached the sand and dropped the rifle. I drew the Bowie, at the same time closing the distance between us. She had fallen, but then she was up and turned to face me with the ax. It was a double-bladed ax, heavy and hard for her to handle. But I told myself to be careful. She could easily split my skull.

As I circled her, the sand squeaking under our feet, neither one of us said a word. The insects were humming madly from the trees, and the moon rode above the bluff, the light casting our shadows on the white sand. I realized she was great with child. That was why she ran so awkwardly.

I moved closer. My plan was to tempt her into swinging the ax. She would never be able to get the heavy head back up quickly enough for another stroke. As she tried, I would close with the Bowie.

She ventured a blow, moving the ax much faster than I expected. The ax passed so close I felt the wind against my face. I moved forward with the Bowie but lost my footing on the sand. As I rose she kicked me in the face with her heel. I rolled away from her and tried to gain my feet. I looked up and saw her standing over me with the ax poised high above her head. As I raised the Bowie to parry the blow, she gave a sharp cry, the first sound I had heard her make, and collapsed on the sand. She placed her hands over her swelling belly.

As I crouched above her, the Bowie raised, I realized the child was the source of her pain. It would be expedient to kill her, but I could not make myself plunge the knife into her heart, not as the child was coming. The living I could kill but not the unborn. I lay beside her on the sand, looking up at the moon over the dark trees and the sprinkling of stars in the sky. I knew the names of the constellations. Strode Maury had taught them to me. She cried out again. Then she spoke.

"Help me," she said.

Her voice was soft and musical.

Suddenly she began to scream, one cry after the other as her body contorted against the movement of the child from her womb. At every scream I thought my heart would break. I wanted to run into the trees, holding my hands about my ears. I forced myself to stay. I brought her water to drink; I bathed her face; I held her hand. I gazed upon her sex. I had not seen a woman since Strode Maury brought me to the house on the river.

The child was born as the sun rose above the trees. I cut the umbilical cord with the Bowie and washed the squalling bloody child in the warm water of the shallows. She suckled it at her breast.

She smiled at me.

Being on the sandbar in the daylight was beginning to disquiet me. I told her that I was going for the pirogue. She looked at me and said nothing.

"I will return, "I said.

"Do as you wish, "she said.

The birds were already circling above the pines on the bluff. Later in the day they would come dropping down through the big trees to feed on the dead man. She was watching the birds also.

"Your husband?" I asked. She shook her head.

She told me that she had escaped from a plantation on the coast. As she wandered the pine forest, the charcoal burner, a free man of color, found her. At the first high water he was intending to take her with him downriver on a raft he was building. He would sell his charcoal on the coast and return her for a reward.

I explained to her who I was and how I was on my way to Haiti. I explained why I had thought it was necessary to kill her.

"I was going to kill him," she said.

I swam the river, retrieving my pistols from where I had dropped them, and climbed the bluff. In the crude cabin the charcoal burner had constructed, I found a tin box containing a little money and his papers. I decided to take on his identity. If people asked questions about the woman, I would say that I was taking her to the coast to claim my reward.

When I brought the pirogue up to the sandbar, she was standing with the baby in her arms by the river's edge.

"Take me to Haiti," she said.

"It will be a difficult voyage," I said. "We could die at sea."

She laughed, a strange sound, which sounded more like the call of a bird than a human cry. "Where else can I go?"

We went down the river a few miles. As was my custom, I ran the boat up into a creek and beached it in a stand of willows. I read the man's papers. He was called Samuel Winthrop. I doubted if he could read his own name. If I were questioned about the papers, I would feign ignorance and my interrogators, assuming I was unlettered, would be impressed that I knew the details contained in them.

Before I went to sleep, I checked the powder pans of the rifle and the pistols. I gave the pistols to the woman whose name, she had told me, was Mary.

"If someone comes into this creek, kill him," I said.

She nodded her head. I believed she would do exactly as I instructed.

We smeared ourselves and the baby with mud against the insects. I went to sleep. Mary held one of the pistols in her lap as she suckled the boy child, brushing the insects away from his face with a willow branch.

I had never felt so tired, not even after I had killed Strode Maury. She was singing a song to the child as she suckled him, her voice cast so low that even as close as I was to her I could not make out the words. I realized that she had not named the child or if she had she had chosen not to reveal the name to me. But I was too exhausted to talk of such matters. They would have to wait until morning. I closed my eyes and slept.

THEY ALL SPECULATED on where the baby had been born, perhaps on one of the sandbars they had already camped on. But Henry pointed out that they were still on the edge of where the longleaf pine forest once began, a little above Monticello.

Robert tried to imagine what it was like to watch the woman give birth on a sandbar. And what it was like for Mary. Robert was still thinking about the Duke in *The White Book*. This time Octavius could easily justify to himself the killing of the charcoal burner. Robert wondered if Octavius was thinking about it that way. Was killing to free someone more acceptable than killing to free oneself? Octavius had killed Strode Maury out of jealousy. To be free himself all he had to do was to have waited for that life in Paris. Robert thought that he would have been justified if he hunted down and killed the men who killed Elaine. But he knew that most people in America would not have approved of personal revenge on his part. Africa was different. It could be that many would have thought it was his duty to take revenge.

Henry got up and left them. He walked to the upstream end of the sandbar, just inside the circle of light, for there were few places on the sandbar where it did not fall. Henry was troubled by the story he had just heard. It sounded too fantastic to be true. He wondered how close the original was to Robert's translation. It seemed to him that if it were true it was all too private. Octavius had hidden the manuscript, so maybe he intended it only for his eyes. But if that were the case he would have written it in code or not written it at all, for he knew the story perfectly well. Perhaps writing it down was his way of trying to understand what had happened to him. There was something else about the narrative that troubled Henry that had nothing to do with whether it was true, but he did not think he could put that something into words. He supposed it had to do with his separation from his tennis partners, a gulf history had placed there.

"What's he doing?" Mason asked.

"Thinking about his people," Robert said.

After a time Henry returned to sit by them. "Are you being careful with the translation?"

"I'm being as careful as I know how."

"Maybe nobody should be translating it. A private thing like that. What went on between those two people."

"I think it should be told," Paul said.

Mason noticed that no one seemed to be expecting him to have an opinion, all of them assuming he would have nothing interesting to say on the subject. He was having trouble understanding why the translation was causing Robert so much difficulty. After all if you knew the words all you had to do was write them down and look up the ones you did not know in the dictionary.

"I don't know why it makes me uneasy," Henry said. "Maybe it's because I know it's not precise. He wrote that years after it happened. Why'd he wait so long? And now even longer after that Robert's translating it. Who knows what really happened?"

"I'm being careful," Robert said. "I didn't add anything, if that's what you mean."

"No, I don't mean that. I can't put a name on what I mean."

"Octavius fell over the edge," Paul observed.

"Yeah," Mason said. "He's out there with them gators."

"Yes," Henry said. "That's what I mean. It doesn't even matter what he does now. He's lost."

"I wonder how he died in Paris," Robert said.

"I've never heard anything about that," said Henry.

"I reckon Robert will have to go to Paris and find out," Mason said.

"He goes down the river killing people to keep himself alive," Paul said. "Then he makes it to Haiti and returns calling himself a Duke. He buys the plantation where he was a slave. I wonder if he went out to Strode Maury's grave. I wonder what he thought if he did that?"

Robert picked up the manuscript. "I could imagine that. I could write it down." He turned to Henry. "Is it all right to do that?"

"Just give us his words," Henry said. "That and nothing else."

"Then that's all I'll do," said Robert.

They talked about Octavius for a long time but reached no definite conclusions. The men went off to sleep, leaving Mason to take the first watch. Paul had moved Hoffman close to the fire where the person on watch could keep an eye on him. Mason sat by the fire, his back against a driftwood log, which he kept between himself and the heat of the fire, the Mannlicher across his knees. He noticed that Hoffman had not gone to sleep but was watching him.

"What you looking at?" Mason said.

Hoffman puffed at his feathers and raised himself to his full height.

Mason wondered if Hoffman remembered being shot. "You know it was me, don't you? Don't worry, I don't shoot tame buzzards." As if in reply Hoffman turned his back to him and put his head under his wing.

Gators grunted from the swamp, and the insects hummed madly. No night birds called. Outside the light the darkness was uniform, a smooth black circle around him.

From time to time Mason got up and made a circuit of the sandbar, a flashlight in his hands. Then he could see the stars and the outline of the cypresses against the lighter darkness of the sky. If he played the light along the river bank, here and there were pairs of red dots, a head or tail transfixed for a moment in the light before the gator scrambled into the darkness. Once he spotted two in the river, swimming across just below the sandbar.

He made a conscious effort to think about Octavius. The teachers were not the only ones who could feel sympathy for what was happening to him. In fact Mason believed he was in a better position than any of them. He wished they would all spend a week living in the trailer and killing trees every day or killing and hanging up chickens at the chicken plant. Ever since that job he had lost all desire to eat chicken. The sight of the naked carcasses hung from overhead hooks and moving through the processing was one that was hard to forget. He expected that his companions would have expected something like that would not have bothered him at all.

Octavius had no light. He had traveled at night among the gators, he and the woman listening to their grunts from this swamp or some other. Octavius must at this point have had little hope he would reach Haiti. The extra burden of the woman and her child was going to make it even more difficult.

At the end of his watch he woke Paul and gave him the rifle.

"Any gators try to come up here?" Paul asked.

"No, your bird's safe."

Paul walked over to Hoffman. "You haven't been bothering him?" He looked at Hoffman who was still asleep, his head under his wing.

"Does he look unhappy? I'm starting to like buzzards as pets. I'm thinking about getting one."

Mason went off to sleep.

Robert, awakened by the changing of the watch, lay in his tent and watched Paul's light as he made a circuit of the sandbar. A gator grunted from across the river, answered by another on the opposite bank. He thought of Octavius, traveling with the woman and the new born child through the darkness, waiting for the light so he could sleep.

Robert closed his eyes and hoped he would dream of them. But when he finally slept he did not dream.

Chapter Nine

LATE IN THE afternoon they reached Monticello. Henry and Mason bought beer and food while Robert and Paul filled the empty gas cans. They sat in the shade of the highway bridge and drank the beer.

"I think we should live like Octavius lived," said Henry.

Mason opened another beer. "We're already doing that."

"He didn't have outboard motors or gas lanterns," Henry said.

"Or cold beer," Paul said.

"Coming close is good enough," Robert said. "I'm not planning on killing anyone either. If Paul wants to cover himself with mud, that's fine. All of us don't have to do it."

"We should have brought muzzle loaders," Henry said. "Do all our hunting with them."

Paul used his knife to take a sausage out of a can. "And we should travel at night."

"No," Robert said. "It's too dangerous. A boat could hit a snag. Someone could end up drowned."

No one supported Paul.

They left the town behind. At dusk they made camp on a sandbar where they ate food out of cans and drank the rest of the beer. Everyone went to sleep early.

In the morning Robert woke to a blue and cloudless sky. Already it was very hot. Once they had broken camp and were underway, he sat under the canopy and worked on the translation.

They went down through a shoals where the river was split by several small islands on which grew thick stands of willows and river birches. It was so shallow they had to walk the boats.

Farther down they came upon several deep pools, shaded by the trees. Here they paused to swim.

Robert and Mason swam a little way from Henry and Paul. Henry had caught a banded water snake. He was showing Paul something about the construction of the snake's mouth.

They floated on their backs. The leaves of the willows rippled in the breeze, but no breeze reached the surface of the pool, which was smooth and black, like a polished piece of metal.

"What'd your daddy do for a living?" Mason asked.

"He was a commercial photographer," Robert said.

"He's dead?"

"Yes."

"Weddings? Prom pictures?"

"Yeah, things like that."

"Daddy mostly drove trucks. And cut some pulp wood. But he was bad to take a drink. Mostly he lay about and did nothing. When he wasn't drunk he hunted and fished. Then he got too sick to do that. I thought your daddy'd be a banker or a lawyer."

"I think—" Robert began.

"Henry, leave that damn thing alone!" Mason shouted.

They looked across the pool at Henry, who had pinned a cottonmouth to the bank with a forked stick. The snake squirmed, throwing coils about the stick.

"Only man I know who catches cottonmouths for entertainment," Robert said.

Henry picked the snake up, holding its head between his thumb and forefinger. The snake threw a coil about his arm. Henry used his free hand to uncoil it. Then the snake hung slack, its tail touching the water, unable to overcome its own weight. Mason swam to the boat. He poled it across the pool to where Henry was standing. Mason held a pistol in his hand.

"Be careful," Henry said, who was still holding the cotton-mouth, its thick body dangling over the water.

Mason raised the pistol and shot the snake in half, leaving Henry holding the upper part.

"You do get yourself worked up," Henry said.

"I want to see every one of those damn things dead," Mason said.

"It'll wear you out doing it. It'll surely wear you out."

Henry tossed the still squirming head into the river. They returned to the boats.

The river curved to the right with low banks on both sides. They approached the end of an island, the open water ahead visible. They were poling the boats across a deep pool, Robert's boat in the lead, when Robert heard something huge slide down the bank. He turned too late to see it as it hit the pool, making a great splash in the dark water.

"Gator?" Mason asked.

"No," Henry said, "*Macrochelys temminckii.*"

"Dammit, Henry," Mason said. "Speak English."

"An alligator snapping turtle. I didn't think one could grow that large."

"How big?" Mason asked.

The boats were now side by side. Ahead of them the pool was dark, most of it lying in the shade of the willows.

"I'd say five-hundred pounds," Henry said. "I don't believe I'm saying that. Maybe two-hundred, but not five hundred. That turtle must be the oldest thing in this river."

"Maybe it was alive when Octavius was here," said Paul.

"Not that old," Henry said. "No animal on this earth lives that long."

"Let's eat it," Mason said.

"I'd say we should leave it alone," said Paul.

"No, it'll feed all of us," Robert said. "How do you catch a turtle like that, Henry?"

Henry shook his head. "Don't know. A big turtle like that could take a man's hand right off."

"I know a way to get that turtle," said Mason.

"Not with dynamite," Paul said.

"I've got a better way."

Mason explained how he and his father caught them by swimming down to a turtle as it rested on the bottom and slipping a noose over its tail.

"It's easy," he said.

"I think we should leave that animal alone," Paul said. "How can we kill something so old."

"I believe I like snapper steaks better than soft shell," Mason said.

"It's near the end of its life," Henry said. "Once it's gone there'll be more room for the little ones. But we need to be careful. I believe that thing could swallow a wood duck in one bite."

Mason put on Henry's fins and mask. He tied a noose in a piece of nylon rope.

"Maybe Henry should do it?" Robert said.

Mason stepped into the water. "I'm going to."

He swam out over the pool, the white line paying out behind him in coils against the dark water. Henry poled the boat after him while Robert stood in the bow and fed him the line. Mason dived to follow the trail of stirred-up sediment left by the turtle.

As the pool deepened, he ran out of air and surfaced. With a determined look on his face, he dove again.

They watched him as he swam into deeper water. Now it was becoming difficult to follow his progress, which was obscured by both the sediment trail and the depth of the water. For time they all felt concern for him. The big turtle could catch him in its beak and not let go. He could drown down there in the darkness. One of them might have to go after him.

Mason surfaced again and treaded water.

"You be careful," Henry cautioned. "He's lying down there in the mud, at the bottom of the deepest place he can find."

He dived, his passage marked by the air bubbles and the flash of his body against the dark water. Then he disappeared; the rope ceased to move.

The boats stopped, and everyone peered down into the water. No one said a word. A woodpecker drummed on a tree; a bird sang beautifully from high in the willows.

Robert prepared to go over the side.

"The rope!" Henry said.

The rope was moving off downstream, at first slowly but now at a faster rate. Mason burst to the surface and took in great gasps of air.

"I got him!" he shouted. "I got him!"

Robert grabbed at the rope, which was rapidly paying out from a coil in the bow. It was like a thing alive and slipped out of his hands, burning them, but he managed to get a grip on it and tie it off to a towing cleat set in the bow.

The boat shot past Mason.

"Damn if he isn't going to tow us to the Gulf!" Henry shouted.

They were past the island now and into the wider river. Behind them he heard the outboard of the other boat start. In a few moments it was beside him.

"How big is that thing?" asked Henry.

"Big as a hog!" Mason shouted.

Ahead was a large sandbar on the right hand side of the river and a bluff on the left. The turtle stopped when it reached a big pool at the foot of the bluff. Henry took the boat into the sandbar.

Robert untied the rope, and they all took hold of it. Like a team in a tug-a-war, they dug their feet into the sand and pulled, but the turtle would not budge.

"Dynamite," Mason said as he sat on the sand breathing hard.

"No," said Paul. "You can't do that."

"Why not?" Mason asked.

"It's just not right," said Paul.

"There'll be no dynamite," Robert said.

Mason stood up and brushed the sand off his clothes. "Then we'll be eating deer jerky tonight."

Henry tied the rope off to the trunk of a willow. They all retreated to the shade and had a drink of water. The rope stretched out into the river, disappearing into the pool. When Robert tugged on it, there was no movement at all. It was as if it were tied to the trunk of a sunken cypress.

"He's dug himself into the mud," Henry explained. "We'd need a jeep with a winch to get him out."

"He'll have to come up to breathe," Robert said. "That's when we'll pull him into the shallow water."

"He can stay down there a long time," Henry said. "Turtles can breathe underwater through their anus and the pharyngeal cavity."

"A what?" Mason asked.

"A sort of gill."

"So how long do you think he'll stay down?" Mason asked.

"A long time. Maybe for days if he wants to."

"Dynamite," Mason said. "That's what he needs. Stir him up some."

"No, we'll wait," Robert said.

They set up camp, leaving the rope tied around the trunk of a willow. Mason stood by the rope for some time, his hand on it, so if the turtle moved he would know. But after an hour he was sitting instead of standing and then he came under the tarp and lay down to sleep.

Robert worked on the translation while the rest ate deer jerky. Then Henry and Mason went to sleep.

Paul took a boat and followed the rope out into the river. He carried Hoffman with him. The bird was content to sit quietly on his perch under the canopy. He tied the boat to a snag and sat there in the bow gazing down at the water, his hand on the rope. Robert finished the translation and watched Paul for a time. He thought about taking the other boat out and talking with him. But it was too hot. Paul, who was bareheaded, sat motionless in the sun. He seemed to take no notice of the heat at all, as if he were down at the bottom of the pool with the turtle and not in the boat at all.

Mason woke up. He walked down to the edge of the water. Paul was sitting in the boat with his back to him. Both Paul and Hoffman were staring at the water.

"Paul, what's that turtle saying?" Mason yelled.

Paul ignored him.

"You say him a poem today?"

Neither Paul nor Hoffman gave any sign that they had even heard Mason.

"What's Hoffman think about it?"

Paul said nothing in reply.

Mason walked back to the tarp. Henry was still asleep.

"What'd you think he's doing?" Mason asked.

"Waiting for the turtle," Robert said.

"Talking to it. That's what he's doing."

"What do you mean, 'talking?'"

"He wakes up in the morning and goes down to the river and talks to the birds and the fish and the snakes. He talks to that buzzard all the time. I've been watching him. He does it when he thinks nobody's watching. He speaks poetry to them. Out of a book sometimes. Out of his head other times. I've seen him do it plenty of times. It's gotten so that I wake up before he does and wait for him to go do it."

"And what do the animals say in return?"

"Dammit, this is serious. That man needs to get off this river."

"What do they say?"

"He won't tell me."

"That's because there's nothing to tell. Paul is playing games. That's all."

"It makes me nervous. You saw him when I shot that vulture. It's the same thing. You remember how he said that we're upsetting the balance by killing things. It's gotten so that I think about that every time I eat a fish or a piece of deer meat. It makes me not want to eat at all sometimes."

"It's not worth thinking about."

"Look at that."

Paul had pulled off his swimming trunks. He lowered himself over the side of the boat.

"Come on," Mason said.

Robert followed Mason to the river's edge. Paul had already made a surface dive, his legs disappearing with a splash. Hoffman had his eyes fixed on the spot where Paul had made the dive. They waited. Mason watched the second hand on his watch. Robert imagined Paul at the bottom of the river, his body slipping past tangles of snags, working his way through the darkness toward the turtle. Henry joined them.

"That boy has got a fine pair of lungs," Mason said.

Paul surfaced. They all called out to him, but he did not answer. He dived again.

"What's he doing?" Mason asked.

Robert wondered if Paul was attempting to release the turtle, but if he had wanted to do that all he had to do was take a knife and cut the rope.

"Look!" Mason said.

The rope had begun to move. Paul had still not emerged.

Hoffman turned his head to watch the moving rope. Henry awakened and walked down to join them.

"That buzzard can see him," Mason said. "That damn thing can see through the water. Him and his polarized eyes."

"Calm down," Henry said. "He can't see him any better than we can."

Mason had his eye on his watch again. "Where's Paul? He'll be out of air by now." Mason continued to watch the second hand of his watch. "More than two minutes. That man's not human."

"The turtle's got him," Henry said. "He'll drown."

"He won't," Mason said. "He's sitting in the mud next to that turtle, breathing through his asshole."

Paul surfaced just beyond the place where the rope disappeared beneath the water. At the same time the rope began to slowly move out of the pool toward the island. They watched the slack sliding across the sand.

"We'll wait until he crosses that bar," Henry said. "Catch him in the shallow water."

Mason ran across the sand to the tree and untied the rope. They all took a grip on it.

Paul stood up in the shallow water at the head of the bluff pool, directly in the path of the turtle. He held a knife in his hand. Hoffman flapped his good wing and shook his head.

"Don't you mess with that turtle!" Mason yelled.

They took up the slack but put no pressure on the turtle. The line was bellied out, the gentle current putting a curve in its center. They all dug their feet into the sand and got ready to pull.

"One, two, three," Mason shouted. "Pull!"

They threw the weight of their bodies against the rope, which was immediately pulled taut, all of them feeling the dead weight of the turtle.

"Pull!" Mason shouted. "Pull!"

They had altered the path of the turtle, pulling it diagonally across the river and into the shallow water. When its serrated shell rose above the water not one of them could not believe it was so large. It shook its ponderous head, the beaked jaw opening wide and exposing the pinkish inside of its mouth.

"We've got him!" Mason shouted. "We've got him!"

But then the turtle lurched forward, its legs flailing, and reached deeper water, pulling all of them across the sand. Mason slipped and fell. He began to curse.

Out in the river Paul, who was standing in knee-deep water, yelled at them. "Too strong for you!"

Everyone strained on the rope, all of them pulling so hard there was no talking or shouting. There were only the sounds of their groans and their breathing. They gained ground and brought the turtle into shallow water again. It was tiring, no longer moving its feet as rapidly. Then, when it moved into the water no more than a foot or so deep, its increased weight stopped them. It could not escape, but they could pull it no closer.

Paul was running through the shallow water, running with his knees high, kicking up water around him. His cock and balls had drawn up small. Robert thought of pictures of Greek athletes. The knife flashed in the sunlight.

"Paul, no!" Henry yelled.

Henry ran through the shallows towards him. Robert ran after him.

There was the crack of the Mannlicher. The turtle's head lurched to one side from the impact of the bullet and blood sprayed. Mason stood on the sandbar behind them, the rifle over his shoulder.

"It's turtle steaks tonight, Paul! " he yelled. "Turtle steaks!"

Paul was crying. Robert put his arm around his shoulder while the others gathered about the turtle.

"Damn you, Mason!" Paul shouted. "Damn you!"

Then Paul turned to Robert. "I was down there with him. He took me in his beak. He swam with me. We swam together." Paul shoved his forearm in front of Robert's face. "See."

There was an impression there, a pair of reddish marks. The marks could been made as Paul climbed over the gunwale of the boat; he could have become entangled with an underwater snag.

"Your arm?" Robert asked.

"Yes, he held me," Paul said. "But gently."

"How did you get away?"

"I did nothing. He released me. I'd run out of air and he released me."

Paul waded into the deep water and swam to the boat. The others ignored him. They, directed by Mason, were intent on butchering the turtle.

"Roll him over," Mason said.

The three of them put their shoulders to the turtle. They all smelled the mud on the turtle's carapace, which was slick with algae. And there was that reptilian stink.

"Heave!" Mason said.

They all pushed but nothing happened.

"Rock him," Mason said.

So they all began to rock the turtle, pushing and then releasing. Robert felt the weight of the animal. In the water the efforts of the three men would have been nothing to the turtle. It was as if all that vanished wilderness was distilled in this one animal, now heavy with time instead of blood and flesh and shell.

"Heave hard!" Mason shouted.

Then the weight was gone as they all pushed, the turtle suspended weightless for a moment on the edge of its shell. The turtle fell with a splash over onto its back. Mason split the plastron open with an ax, removed the guts, and then began to cut steaks off the turtle. By now it was dark, and they worked by lantern light. Paul remained in the boat.

Mason and Henry grilled the steaks over the coals. They all tried to persuade Paul to come and eat, but he still sat with his back to them and did not reply.

"At least give that buzzard something to eat," Mason yelled.

Hoffman flapped his good wing and moved back and forth on his perch. Paul reached out and stroked his head, and Hoffman calmed down.

"Paul?" Mason called.

"Leave him alone," Henry said.

"Let him sleep out there then. The mosquitoes'll eat him alive."

They all ate turtle steaks and drank whiskey. Soon Robert forgot that Paul was sitting out in the boat in the darkness. Mason did not taunt him again; no one mentioned Paul's name.

Robert concentrated on the meat. When he finished one steak, Henry put another one on his plate. Robert pushed the meat into his mouth and chewed it carefully. Henry and Mason ate as they cooked. No one talked. They filled their mouths with the meat, which did not have the sort of musky taste they expected. Instead, as they each chewed a mouthful, no one thought it held a wild flavor. It simply tasted ancient.

Chapter Ten

They were waiting by the fire for Robert to read his translation. They had turned off all the lanterns except one to save fuel. He had walked across the sand to the water's edge and was calling to Paul. Robert could see, illuminated by the starlight, the outline of Paul's body, an erect and motionless form. Hoffman had his head tucked under his wing. Robert called again, but still Paul did not reply.

"Leave him be," Henry called. "I want to read it," he added.

Robert handed him the manuscript. Henry began to read.

Our Freedom Is Challenged

We traveled for three nights, sleeping in the pirogue during the day. Mary complained that the mosquitoes were troubling the child even though we had plastered him with mud as we had ourselves. I told her that if she wanted the child to be free we all would have to endure privations. She had named him John. She was Catholic and longed for the child to be baptized.

I was working the pirogue down through a garden of snags in a thick, rich darkness, the stars and moon blocked by clouds. Now and then there was the rumble of thunder in the distance, and the clouds were faintly illuminated by lightning.

I could barely see Mary and the child in the bow of the pirogue. I heard the sound of his greedy lips at her breast.

The river bent to the right. I took the boat to the outside of the bend where there was the most current. I slid the boat over a log and then turned to avoid the bole of an uprooted tree whose trunk lay downstream and parallel with the current. As I made the turn, the pirogue caught on a snag with a thump and a grinding noise and tilted to one side, pitching Mary and the child into the river. Neither of them made a sound. There was only the splash of their bodies hitting the water. The boat was still upright, for I had caught it with the pole.

Mary screamed for the child, and I knew that she had lost him. I went over the side and closed my hand around an arm, which I realized was Mary's, and released it at the same instant. Then I was past her, the current carrying me down river as my outstretched fingers groped in that absolute darkness, searching for the child. Then, just as I was running out of air, I felt his leg and seized it. I kicked for the surface, holding the child above my head in my outstretched arms so that he reached the air before me, and when I burst through, taking in great gulps of air, he was wailing, a cry of life.

She demanded that we stop, that there be no more traveling at night and that we camp on high ground. She could not keep the stinging and biting insects from the child's tender body. And I complied. I put the pirogue ashore at the first bluff we passed and make a camp at the top among the big pines. We built a fire of pine knots. There was a breeze this night and the tops of the pines soughed in it. The insects were not so bad.

She and the child slept soundly, but I could not sleep. I stood out in the trees, away from the light of the fire, with the rifle in my hands. I stayed there until the glow of the embers disappeared and the bluff was in absolute darkness. Then in that sort of early morning false dawn, when the sky appeared to lighten, but I knew it was hours to true light, I lay down beside the woman and child and slept, the rifle cradled in my arms.

Mary's breasts were full of milk, and I wanted to keep them that way. She needed rich food. I awoke with the rising sun and shot a deer that had come down the drink at the sandbar on the other side of the river.

After I butcherd the deer, I crossed to the bluff and gave her a haunch of venison, which she began to cook over a fire. I gave her the pistols. I returned to the sandbar to smoke the meat. I planned to spend one more day and night at this place and then go down river with a supply of cured deer meat. Even if my hunting and fishing went poorly, she and the child would stay strong.

At midday I was sitting in the shade watching the meat cure when I saw through the branches of the willows a big pirogue coming up the river. Three men were in it and as it drew closer I made out two Indians and one white man. He was a priest, his dark clothes in contrast to

*their naked bodies. I thought that it must be fear-
fully hot in those clothes. Only his broad-
brimmed black hat would give him any relief from
the sun.*

*They knew someone was on the sandbar be-
cause of the smoke. The Indians no doubt had
rifles in the pirogue. I considered killing the
stern paddler. The priest might or might not be
a warrior priest. I thought that if I shot the stern
paddler, the others would be thrown into confu-
sion. I would have time to reload and kill the
other one, unless he went into the water. I considered how difficult a head shot would be, particularly since the current would be bearing him
away from me.*

*Then I suddenly found I had no choice at all,
because Mary was standing on the bluff with the
baby in her arms. She was calling to the priest.
She had put on her dress so as not to offend him
with her nakedness. She called again, her voice
shrill and urgent. She held out the child to him.*

*The Indian in the bow picked up his rifle,
looking not at Mary but at the trees behind her.
The other Indian stood up in the bow, balancing
himself with the paddle like a man on a wire.
The priest sat stiffly as if he had been cut from a
piece of thick black paper. He raised his hand to
her. I thought that if I had two rifles I could kill
both of them. They were too far away for pistols.*

*I stepped out from behind the screen of wil-
lows. The Indian in the stern dropped his paddle
and picked up a rifle. The priest turned and spoke
to him. The Indian sat down. Both of them took
up their paddles and quickly closed the distance*

between us. I stood with the rifle cradled in my hands.

The Indian in the bow asked me if I was a free man. I told him I was. The Indian in the stern laughed and said that the rifle made me free. Yah, the man in the bow said, no slave would be allowed to have a rifle. Then the priest asked me for my papers. I told him the papers were at the camp on the bluff. I told him that Mary was a runaway slave and that I was taking her back to claim my reward. I told him that I was hopeful that I would be paid extra for delivering the child.

I poled my pirogue across the river and climbed the bluff with the men, wondering if my ruse with the bear convinced anyone or if handbills advertising my escape had been posted everywhere.

Mary met us at the top of the bluff with the child in her arms. She implored the priest, whose name was Father Lucian, to baptize him. He smiled at her and promised he would. I did not believe that the priest was armed. If anything went wrong, I would kill one of the Indians immediately with the rifle and close upon the other with my knife. Then I would deal with the priest. It was beginning to seem to me that my journey was being paid for with dead men. At some point, even if I reached Haiti, there would be some sort of reckoning for what I had done.

The priest read the paper granting me my freedom. 1 prayed that he did not personally know the man who wrote the document and asked me questions I would be unable to answer. He asked me questions, assuming as I hoped he would that I was unlettered, and I answered to his satisfaction. Mary pressed him to baptize the child.

He agreed to do so. We all went down to the river. He took a wooden case out of the pirogue and removed a vial of holy water. He said the Latin words over the child. The Indians, Samuel and Isaac, watched, standing at some distance, but close enough to hear his words. Their greased bodies glistened in the sun.

Then we returned to the bluff. Mary nursed the child while the priest asked me questions about what I had seen upriver. He was searching for a group of unbaptized Indians who had not left the country according to a recent treaty. They had hidden themselves away, deep in the longleaf pine forest. He wanted to convert them. Samuel and Isaac were members of their tribe. He told me that God appeared to him in a vision and informed him of the existence of the Indians and commanded him to undertake the mission.

I went across the river and finished the job of curing the meat. I packed it in a basket Mary had woven of sweet grass. Father Lucian bathed in the river wearing all his clothes. For a long time he stood in a pool with just his head above water.

That night we feasted on the deer and then full of food we all prepared to sleep. Father Lucian told us that the Indians would stand watch. He had picked them out on the street in Biloxi, another miracle. He recognized them instantly as members of the tribe in his vision. He gave them their Christian names that day as they knelt before him in the mud, astonished and amazed by the power of God.

I pretended to go to sleep, and soon I was listening to the Father Lucian's snores. Mary waked by my side to the mews of the baby and suckled him. Then mother and child slept. The fire burned down; we were left in darkness. Once one of the Indians walked through the camp, his feet noiseless on the thick accumulation of needles. I closed my eyes and slept.

I woke at sunrise to the pain of someone's knee in my back. My hands were being bound with rawhide thongs. It was the Indians. Mary began to wail. I smelled cigar smoke. They pulled me to my feet. I expected to see the priest lying dead on the ground, but instead he stood, his cassock bunched up under his arms, urinating into the ashes of the fire, the ashes hissing as the stream of urine hit them. He held a cigar clenched between his teeth.

He walked over to me and told me he was no priest. He was a catcher of runaway slaves. A priest interfered with his lawful practice of his profession and he, Angus Thompson, killed him. He told me that he looked into the eyes of the dying priest for a long time to see if the priest would give some sign that he was in the presence of God, but there was nothing, no sign. He died like any man, Angus told me. Like a deer or a bear.

Angus talked to me, not expecting I would understand or that the Indians or Mary would understand, as if he were talking before an assembly of dogs or horses. He told me that he had learned his Latin for a career as a lawyer, which he later abandoned. At night he read

*Shakespeare to the Indians, who listened in ab-
ject and total incomprehension.*

*I protested I was a free man. The paper
proved it. He said that he believed me to be the
escaped slave who had killed Strode Maury. He
pulled a bill out of his pocket and shoved it before my face. It was a description of me. You
can read it well, can't you, he said. That man
taught you your letters and you killed him for
it. You are the devil's spawn. He deserved what
he got, being so foolish as to teach a nigger to
read.*

*The child began to cry. There was a pistol
shot and we turned to see Samuel fall. Isaac
brought his rifle up, but Mary shot him with the
other pistol. Angus sprang for his rifle. I butted
him to the ground with my head. I threw myself
on top of him and fastened my teeth about his
throat, which tasted of salt and smoke. I
searched for his windpipe with my teeth. He
reached for my eyes with his fingers. I closed
them tight, his fingers clutching at the lids. I
clenched my jaws on his throat as I tried to
pinch off his windpipe. Suddenly he gave a little
cry, and his hands fell away from my face. I
opened my eyes. Mary had driven the point of
the Bowie through his left eye and into his
brain.*

*I told her that we could no longer travel in
the daytime or camp in such exposed places.
From now on we would be creatures of the
swamps and creeks, places so full of snakes and
insects that few would want to venture there.*

*Mary nodded her head grimly in agreement.
We collected their weapons. The slave hunter*

had a set of pistols concealed under his cas-
sock along with a Bowie knife. We left their
bodies for the birds.

"HE'S STILL NOT going to let us inside," Henry said. "It's like he's a camera, just recording the events."

"What should be he telling us?" Mason said. "I don't understand why you want so much from him. Maybe he don't even know what he's feeling. Maybe he wrote it so long afterward that he forgot."

"It could be that he just can't tell it all," Robert offered. "Or he doesn't want to. I don't think we're going to see the interior of this man."

Robert considered how he had no inclination to tell his companions of the death of his wife and his reaction to it. He wondered if it would be possible for him to describe precisely how he felt during the long winter he spent alone in the house. Elaine had been killed just before Christmas. He supposed that a man like his teacher Peter would have been able to do that. He could tell them about his flirtation with suicide. The details of it would be easy to relate. And maybe they were wrong and Octavius was right. It could be that all that was necessary was to relate exactly what had occurred, leaving out no detail. That interior life was too confused, too chaotic for anyone to make sense of.

"Have you read ahead into it?" Henry asked.

Robert shook his head. "No, I'm going by the rules."

Robert imagined that Octavius could have had little hope he would reach Haiti. With the lure of a reward everyone along the river would be looking for him. The closer he drew to the Gulf the more searchers there would be.

"I'd never let them take me alive," Henry said. "Me, or the woman and the child."

"What? Kill them?" Robert asked.

"Better to be dead than slaves," said Henry.

Henry considered those people who absolutely refused to be

slaves. The intractable ones who were killed or killed themselves, but for most the desire to live trumped everything.

"And what of the child?" Robert asked. "That child has no choice."

"I agree with Henry," Mason said. "Better to be dead."

Mason was surprised at how interested he had become in the suffering of Octavius as the narrative had proceeded. It seemed to him that he had more in common with Henry than with Robert. He thought he understood how Henry felt. Robert's life had been too comfortable to allow him to really understand the depths of Octavius' desperation.

They built up the fire and sat around it for a long time talking about how Octavius might proceed.

"He did it," Robert said. "You need to remember that he did it. He reached Haiti."

"But we don't know about the woman and her child," Henry said. "Robert, are you sure you haven't read ahead?"

"I haven't," Robert said. "We'll all have to wait."

Henry went off to sleep. Robert walked out of the circle of firelight and down to the river's edge. He called out to Paul but received no answer. Mason came up beside him.

"Is he still there?" he asked.

"Yes," he said.

Mason started to turn his flashlight on him.

"No, leave him alone."

They stood together for a time, looking off into the darkness.

"When I was a boy I was wild to learn to shoot," Robert said. "We were living in Atlanta. I'd go out to the Peachtree Gun Club. Watch them shoot skeet and trap. My father hated guns and hunting. His father made him sit in duck blinds out on Lake Ponchatrain when he was a boy. He never liked the killing. But he could sure blow a duck call. Couldn't shoot worth a lick, but he could call ducks."

"How about you?"

"Not like he could. I was practicing one day and I guess he got tired of hearing it done so badly. He came out on the back porch and showed me how. It was like magic what that man could do with a duck call."

"Did he like taking all them pictures?"

"Those weddings. Those portraits of children. No, I don't think so. I think he wanted to be some other kind of photographer. Maybe take pictures of ducks. But he never did. He got sick. It was a tumor in his liver. He shot himself. One shot in the head with my mother's little Beretta she carried in her purse. They'd argue about that gun. But she wouldn't give it up and went to the range once a week to practice."

"She was a smart woman."

"Maybe she was. I don't know. Sometimes I wish my father had gotten himself to Louisiana one winter. Gone out on the lake and called ducks into a set of decoys and took pictures of them."

Mason looked off into the darkness towards Paul's boat. "I reckon Daddy would've been happy cat fishing on the river. He liked that about as well as anything."

"I do that translation and I can't quite believe what I'm reading," Robert said. "I'm afraid for Octavius, for what's happening to him. He's trapped. Reading it makes me feel trapped too."

"None of us is trapped. We can all go home anytime we want."

"I'm not leaving the river until we reach the Gulf."

"Yeah, everybody gets to do whatever they want." Mason yawed. "I'm going to sleep." He pointed out towards Paul. "What about him? He's acting crazy."

"Maybe tomorrow he'll come back to us," Robert said. Mason turned and walked back to the fire.

Robert remained by the river. As his eyes adjusted to the dark, he made out the shape of the boat and Paul and Hoffman's shapes too. He wondered if Paul had heard every word he and Mason had said. They had not considered how well their voices might carry across the water.

"Paul, what are you doing out there?" Robert called, his voice sounding unusually loud in the darkness.

There was no reply. "Are you all right?"

"Go to sleep," Paul replied.

His voice was as clear as if he had been standing where Mason had stood. "You need to sleep too. You can't sleep in the boat."

"I'm not sleepy."

"There're gators out there."

"I'm not worried about gators."

"You want company?"

"No."

"Just tell me what you're doing."

Paul did not reply. Robert considered taking the boat and going out to him, but decided against it.

"Paul?" Robert called, louder than was necessary.

The only response was silence. He heard the gurgle of the river against the hull of Paul's boat.

He stood there for a time, looking for any movement, but Paul and Hoffman were like statues someone had placed in the boat. Finally the mosquitoes began to bother him and he went to his tent to sleep.

Chapter Eleven

THEY WOKE IN the morning to find Paul, naked and plastered with mud, perched atop the turtle's shell, the painter from the boat tied around his waist. The boat rested just downstream, the gentle current causing it to tug against the painter. Hoffman sat beside him. Paul was feeding Hoffman turtle meat. Paul reached down and with his knife sliced off another piece of meat. On snags in the river and in the top of a dead pine, the vultures waited. They all called out to Paul, but he refused to answer.

"It's like God has laid His hand on that man," Mason said.

Robert walked out from under the tarp and across the sandbar. The vultures on the snags watched him warily, nervously spreading and unspreading their wings. The birds stayed put until he put his foot in the water. Then they took flight in their awkward manner and joined their fellows in the dead pine. Robert walked through the warm, knee-deep water and reached Paul. A great swarm of flies buzzed around him, searching for places to lay their eggs in the meat.

"Come get some breakfast," Robert said.

Paul looked bad. His eyes were shot through with red. There was a cut on his arm, a long slash.

"Wash that mud off you," Robert said. "Put on some clothes. Get some breakfast."

Paul didn't appear to be listening. He was watching the birds in the trees. "They're splendid. Light, you know. Hollow-boned. Lighter than air."

A vulture took off from the tree and sailed out over the river. The men, along with Hoffman, watched the bird's wings quiver as it adjusted to pockets of rough air over the water.

"I swam in the river this morning," Paul said. "I saw with a crayfish's eye. I saw everything. God, it was wonderful! I'll tell Elizabeth! She'll know too!"

"Come get some breakfast."

"Melons?"

"Fish and grits. Henry set out some lines last night."

"I'd like that."

Paul slid off the shell and walked into the deeper water and began washing the mud off his body.

"Put some clothes on."

Robert could imagine Paul hallucinating out there in the darkness from solitude and lack of sleep. That was all he needed, sleep and human company. Paul pulled the boat to him. He put on a pair of swimming trunks. He removed Hoffman from the shell and put him on his perch. Then Paul took the boat down to the sandbar.

Robert waded back, reaching the sandbar before Paul did.

"You ease up on Paul," Robert said to Mason. "He's in a bad way."

"Paul should go home," Mason said.

Henry poured Robert a cup of coffee. "He can get off the river at Columbia."

"He needs sleep," Robert said. "He'll be fine. He can leave if he wants."

"What that boy needs is to take up hang gliding," Mason said. "Then he can fly around all day long with them buzzards."

"None of that talk when he comes back," Robert said.

Paul beached the boat on the sandbar. He walked up to them smiling.

"I'm hungry," he said.

"We'll get you some breakfast," said Mason.

"I'll be catching shrimp when the river gets tidal," Henry said. "All the shrimp you can eat."

"And oysters," Mason added.

Mason filleted the catfish, rolled the pieces in flour, and fried them in oil over the gas stove. Henry prepared a pot of grits.

Paul was talking rapidly, describing what he called the "insides of things."

"I swam in a minnow's eye," Paul said. "I rode in a gar's belly. Dragonflies fanned me with their wings."

Mason left him alone. No one mentioned the turtle.

Soon Paul was talking only to Henry, who strolled with him to the down stream end of the sandbar. They stood together at the edge of the water.

"Henry, the world is not what it seems to be," Paul said.

"Maybe, but science is the only way to know what it is," Henry replied.

"Through grass."

"Yes, that method, but not the poet's."

"I was down there with that turtle. I know."

"What happened?"

"I can't explain it. You can't explain something like that with words."

"Try."

"It was like I could breathe water instead of air. That's how I stayed down so long."

"Show me, right now."

Henry was sorry for the words the moment they came out of his mouth. This was not the way to deal with Paul. Right now he was too fragile.

Paul looked down at the water flowing by at their feet.

"I can't do it again. The turtle showed me how. He took me by the arm. Now he's dead."

Yes, Henry thought. *And we ate him.* "You can't go back to that. You going to have to live in this world."

"I suppose. You know, Henry, I feel better now. You made everything so clear. You must be a good teacher."

Then Paul walked off to tend to Hoffman.

They broke camp and were on the river again. Before long Paul had gone to sleep beneath the canopy.

"Nothing but lack of sleep," Henry said. "That's all."

It was a day of intense heat. They saw no game. On both sides of the river were cypress swamps or thick stands of oaks and hickories. Then the land was higher and there were pines again.

Robert sat beneath the canopy and worked on the translation. Most of the time they were under power. The next day or the following one they would reach Columbia.

At lunch they ate what little was left of the jerky and drank warm water. Mason fished with a cast net but had no luck. Out on the river again, they traveled for miles without seeing even a wading bird or a cattle egret. Paul was asleep again. Everyone was hungry and irritable. Robert tried to shut out the heat and their bickering and concentrate on the translation.

"A deer," Mason said.

Robert looked up from his work and saw something ahead on a midstream sandbar.

"It's a dog," Henry said.

Mason took up the Mannlicher and looked through the scope. "Somebody's lost a coonhound."

The dog was overjoyed to see them. He was a black and tan coonhound wearing a blaze-orange collar. He was sleek and healthy and looked as if he could run for days. He danced about wagging his tail and begging to be petted. The dog sniffed at Hoffman who in response drew himself up to his full height and hissed and clacked his beak. Paul continued to sleep.

"That's a purebred coonhound," Mason said. "Somebody paid a lot of money for that dog."

On the collar were a name and a phone number. "We'll call when we get to Columbia," Henry said.

"Are we going to take him with us?" Mason asked.

"No," Robert said. "Somebody was running dogs around here last night. Right now they're probably looking for him. They'll be blowing horns or whistles."

Everyone stood silent and listened. There was only the far off sound of a solitary crow.

"I don't hear anything," Mason said.

"We can't just leave him," said Henry.

"We'll call and let them know where he is," Robert said.

Robert was glad that Paul was still asleep, sleeping as if he were drugged. Paul would have most likely made a passionate argument for taking the lost dog with them.

They left the dog on the sandbar. For a few moments the animal watched the boats drifting with the current, all of them turned to watch him. When the distance increased to thirty yards, the dog bounded into the water and began to swim after them. If they had been under power, they would soon have pulled away from him, but since they were poling he kept pace with the progress of the boats.

"Looks like he's going with us," Mason said.

Henry stopped his boat and waited for the dog to catch up. He went over the side, standing in the waist-deep water, and lifted the dog into the boat where it braced itself unsteadily on the grooved metal bottom and shook, spraying water on Robert. Paul woke up. He petted the dog and tried to introduce him to Hoffman, but the dog shied away from the bird.

"That dog could swim to Haiti," Mason said.

"We'll call him Haiti," said Paul.

Everyone agreed that was a good name.

They continued down the river, stopping now and then to let Mason try his hand with the cast net, while Henry and Paul used spinning rods, but no one had any luck. Henry caught one small bass hardly bigger than the crank bait he was using. Once Mason offered to shoot a cattle egret when they passed a dead tree full of them, but no one was interested in eating one. Robert expected they would have a chance to shoot a deer around sunset.

"We can always use Mason's dynamite," Henry said.

Mason shook his head.

"No, sir," he said. "I'm saving it."

"For what?" Henry asked.

Mason just grinned in reply.

Robert tried drifting along the bank and fishing with the bow, but he only saw schools of minnows and a few bream and small gar.

They passed a long hot afternoon on the river that was mostly too shallow to run the motors and bordered by cypress swamps, so there was no cultivation of any sort going on.

Until it grew dark they remained on the river, for Robert was convinced they would surprise a deer come down to drink off one of the sandbars. But they saw nothing. A few cattle egrets flew overhead, their white feathers gilded by the setting sun.

Finally they gave up and made camp on a sandbar. Everyone bathed in the river and drank some water. Then Henry suggested they eat frog legs for dinner. All they had to do was drift along and play a light along the bank. He would shoot them with a scoped .22. He had hunted frogs that way before. Mason said that he did not care for frog legs. Paul refused to go but gave no reason. He was calm now. He sat on the sand petting Haiti.

So they left Paul and Mason and the dog and hunted frogs. Henry sat in the bow while Robert sculled the boat upstream and used a headlamp he wore to illuminate the bank.

"Do you think Paul is mad?" Robert asked. "What did he say to you?"

"Crazy stuff," Henry said.

"What sort of stuff?"

"Visions he had when he was down there with that turtle. He said the turtle taught him to breathe like a fish. But now he says can't do it anymore."

"I hope that's what he believes. I wonder if that's a good sign. I don't want to have to explain to Elizabeth how we let him drown himself."

But after two hours they had bagged only one frog. They saw a couple of alligators, several raccoons, and many snakes but very few bullfrogs.

"Tough for frogs in this river," Henry said. "If the gators don't get 'em the snakes do."

The river was shallow. They had poled the boats upstream to hunt. Now they drifted back downstream. The night was perfectly clear, and the moon had set, leaving the sky filled with stars. They heard a train whistle. The tracks paralleled the river all the way to the coast and then turned west to New Orleans.

"I'll get up before sunrise and shoot a deer," Robert said.

"Maybe we can talk Mason out of his last stick of dynamite," said Henry.

As they drifted along in the darkness, everyone was silent. Far away whippoorwills were calling, the sound fading in and out. Finally Robert could no longer hear them.

"Can you still hear the birds?" Robert asked.

"Yes," Henry said. "Barely."

The boats drifted in silence.

"There," Henry said, "they're gone."

They caught the scent of meat cooking.

"They shot a deer," Robert said.

"We heard no shot," Henry observed.

"Mason could have used a twenty-two. He would do something like that."

It would not matter to Mason that he would be likely to wound a deer instead of killing it cleanly. They had camped at the foot of a pine-covered bluff. Robert could imagine Mason going up into the pines with a flashlight to jacklight deer. Perhaps a mile or so within the pines was an open field, and he had killed one there.

As they drifted around a bend, they saw the light from the lanterns reflected against the tree trunks of the opposite shore. The air was filled with the scent of cooking meat.

"He's barbecuing it," Henry said. "Maybe Mason finally shot a hog."

"Or stole one," Robert said.

They beached the boats. Just outside the circle of light Paul sat in the boat with Hoffman. Mason was sitting beside the fire. They ran up toward the fire, through air rich with the scent of the meat. Henry was the first to reach the fire.

"Where's Haiti?" Henry shouted. "Mason, what have you done?"

"Fixed you dinner," Mason said.

"Mason's cooking the dog!" Henry said. "You bastard!"

They all came into the firelight. Mason had something on a spit. He was applying the sauce with a paintbrush. He poured whiskey into an aluminum cup and offered it to Henry.

"Have a drink and calm down, Henry," Mason said. "It ain't a dog. It's a coon. He held up the skin. "That dog run off. Swam the river and took off into the trees."

They all sat down around the fire and had a drink of whiskey. Paul came up to the fire.

"Read us what you translated today?" Henry asked.

"After we eat," Robert said.

So they sat and watched the meat cook and drank more whiskey. No one talked much. Every now and then Mason basted the meat.

Paul told a story about how he learned to swim in a creek near his house. He told it lucidly and clearly and everyone laughed at the way he had surprised his father by diving down to the bottom of the pool on the very first try. His father had thought he was drowning and had gone in after him to discover Paul sitting cross-legged on the bottom with a smile on his face.

When the meat was done everyone except Paul, who refused to eat and ate grits instead, devoured it. They ate it all. And when the meat was gone they cracked the big leg bones open and sucked the marrow out of the them.

They went off to bed, full of meat and whiskey. No one suggested to Robert that he read the translation.

Robert went to sleep in his tent, lying naked and flat on his back, his belly full of meat. Then he drifted off to sleep while outside the shrill, mindless rasp of the insects dominated the night.

Chapter Twelve

ROBERT WOKE AT first light to a tent full of mosquitoes. The door was partially unzipped. He crawled out of the tent, wondering how he had forgotten to close it properly.

The birds were just starting to sing; the river was covered with mist. Paul and Henry stood at the down river end of the sandbar. Paul was pacing back and forth with something in his hand. It was the manuscript. Paul must have come in during the night and removed it from the waterproof bag. He had resealed the bag, but he had been careless with the door.

Robert walked across the sand toward Paul. Paul was talking, his eyes away from the manuscript, as if he were an actor memorizing the lines of a script.

"He knows it!" Henry said.

Paul looked rested. His eyes were clear; he was freshly shaved. He had probably bathed in the river and then had heated water over the gas stove for shaving.

"That's all you needed," Robert said. "Just some sleep."

"Some people believe that Homer held the entire Odyssey in his head," Henry said.

"I've heard that," Robert said. "It would have been easier if it were poetry. But why did you do it?"

"So it can never be lost," Paul said.

"I have a copy at home," Robert said. "The original is in a safe deposit box in Jackson. I could always do the translation again. It'd be easy the second time, maybe better."

"It's safe with me," Paul said.

"He can give you any part of it," Henry said. "I've tested him."

Robert could not imagine what harm memorizing the manuscript might do. At least Paul was no longer having visions.

"I want to speak the new chapter this morning," Paul said. "I've got it."

"If that's what you want to do," Robert said.

When Mason woke up, he refused to believe that Paul had memorized the manuscript.

"It ain't possible," he kept saying.

When they all gathered under the tarp for a breakfast of grits and coffee, Paul proved that Henry was right. He stood up before the group and began to talk. Robert held the manuscript before him and followed Paul's recitation.

The Swamp

The child burned with a fever. It frightened me that instead of crying he was silent. He breathed fast as Mary fanned him with a fan she had woven out of stalks of cane. In the narrow creek the mosquitoes hovered in clouds so thick I could see the fan part them as she moved it above the child's face. I smeared more mud on the child's body. I dug deep into the creek bank to find mud that would be cool and soothing to him.

The insects were loud from the thick wall of cane on either bank, their shrieks pitched so high I could imagine them breaking apart and falling to the ground like broken toys. I wanted to stop my ears with mud so I would no longer be able to listen to them. I looked at Mary who fiercely

*hovered over the child, moving the fan with a
regularity that was disturbing. It was as if there
were no connection between her thought of moving the fan and its moving; it was as if she were
a sort of machine.*

*A horn blew, three long blasts, a pure sort of
man sound that for an instant I welcomed, but
then it produced nothing in me but terror. And
far away I heard the dogs. I crouched in the
pirogue beside Mary, my hand on her shoulder,
and listened as the sound came closer. I told her
I thought the dogs were on the other side of the
river, but she said no. The sound swung away
from us, and I was certain the dogs were running on the other bank*

*She asked me what they were running. I told
her it was not men. It was a bear or a panther.
The sound was not right for a deer. These dogs
were running something large and dangerous.
The sound faded and then disappeared. The horn
blew again, one long clear note. She asked me
again if the dogs were running men. I shook my
head.*

*We sat in the pirogue, the whine of the in-
sects washing over us, and listened for the baying. She told me that she heard it, but I shook
my head. Then gradually the sound appeared
beneath the whine, rose, then dominated it.
Whatever the dogs were running was headed
straight toward us.*

*She told me that we must return to the river.
I shook my head. I explained that we must not be
caught on the water in the daylight. But we could
not remain in the creek. If the hounds' quarry
swam the river, the dogs and the men would fol-*

low. The hounds, if they were casting about for the trail, would find us.

I poled the pirogue up the creek. We made a turn and the sound of the dogs was muffled some. Then the creek widened, opening up into a cypress swamp. I was grateful, for this was a place where we could hide. It was not likely the hounds' quarry would come here. At nightfall we could return to the river.

The cypresses were huge, the black water studded with knees. The pirogue cut a trail through patches of green duckweed. I took out the compass and followed a bearing into the swamp. I wanted to make sure we did not become lost in the labyrinth of trees.

The swamp was like one of those cathedrals I had read about but had never seen. Instead of incense, it was filled with the smell of mud and water and trees. Everywhere there were verdant carpets of duckweed. Cypress cones littered the water, and depressions in the buttresses of the trees were filled with accumulations of brown needles. It was quiet. We had left the whine of the insects behind. Dragonflies darted about. A few birds sang; a woodpecker drummed against a tree. An alligator moved off slowly at our approach.

I took the boat behind one of the largest trees. A hole just above the top of a buttress led into its hollow trunk. As I tied off the bow and stern to knees, the dogs drifted off toward the north. They had crossed the river above the creek. The sound faded and then all was silent. We sat in the shade and waited for the afternoon to advance into dusk. Once it was close to dark, I would take a compass bearing and return us to the river. Mary was listening for the dogs. I comforted her; I told her we were safe.

Here we were not tormented by mosquitoes, but I expected that as soon as night fell they would be upon us. Mary suckled the child and rocked him in her arms, singing a song beneath her breath. We went over the side from time to time to cool our bodies. I held the child in my arms and bathed him in that black water. He burned with the fever. Mary took him from me and held him to her breast, rocking gently back and forth and singing.

Toward the end of the afternoon the child died. I knew when it happened because Mary stopped singing. For a few moments neither of us moved, each of us as still as the child. We held our breath, waiting for the child to twist in her arms as he was tormented by the fever or to make a sound. But the child did not move; he did not cry. A breeze stirred the top of the big cypress and a few cones plopped down into the water; a woodpecker drummed upon a tree.

She began to cry soundlessly until her face was wet and shining. Then she stopped. She did not wipe the tears from her face or begin to gasp for breath. She just stopped, as if she had simply run out of tears. She began to sing that song again, even more softly now. I saw her lips moving, but I could not hear the words.

I stepped across the pirogue and put my arms around her. I felt the singing in her body and heard it faintly, but I could not distinguish the words. I felt as if I were nowhere close to her, that she had gone across some great calm gulf and disappeared from my sight into the darkness. I sat for a long time with my arms about her, listening to the songs of the birds and the drumming of a woodpecker. *Every now and then I believed I could hear the baying of the dogs.*

Finally I moved to take the child from her. She offered no resistance. Then she spoke. She told me she was thankful the child had been baptized, that she would constantly pray for his soul. I thought of the false priest and his mock baptism. I told her I believed the child's soul was already in heaven, for the innocent babe had had no opportunity to sin. And I considered the state of my own soul and wondered how I would account for the men I had killed. I had already damned myself with Strode Maury, even before I murdered him.

She poled the boat about the swamp and began to gather Spanish moss. Soon there was a heap of it in the boat. I did nothing. I sat on the bottom of the boat, the marks of the adze used to hew it rough against my legs, and held the child.

Then she poled us back to the big tree. She told me she wished the child to be buried in the tree, lying on a bed of moss. Now we heard the dogs again, swinging back down from the north towards us. Their voices had taken on a frenzied urgency, which made me believe they had drawn close to whatever they were pursuing.

I climbed up into the hole and discovered that the tree was mostly hollow. Lightning had struck it. There was the smell of charred wood. I found a hollow pocket where a wood duck had made a nest and lined it with down. Colorful feathers were everywhere.

I enlarged the pocket with my knife and then lined it with the moss, which she handed up to me. She asked me if it would be a good dry place. I told her it was. She asked me if he would be safe from animals. She said that she could not bear the thought of animals disturbing the burial. And I said that the water would protect the child. It would be as if he were in a castle. But she still worried and asked me to seal up the opening.

We did it with mud, which she brought up from the bottom of the swamp in handfuls. Now the sound of the dogs was much closer. They were on our side of the river. But I was not concerned, for it would be difficult for them to scent us over the water. I squeezed the water out of the mud and built a wall over the opening. Then she discovered a vein of a thick clay, which worked even better. I was able to quickly build a wall, sealing the opening.

Together we knelt in the boat, and she prayed for the child. The baying was coming from near the mouth of the creek. Then it dropped off and stopped altogether. The horn blew again; the hunters called to each other. She continued to pray for the soul of the child, saying her Hail Marys over and over and over.

I heard something swimming through the swamp. As I picked up the rifle, I saw two panthers coming toward us. Their ears were laid back. Bits of white foam clung to their mouths. They had been run long and hard by the dogs. Mary saw them too. She continued to pray.

From the mouth of the creek came more shouts from the hunters. I was thankful we had remained in the pirogue, that there were no tracks on the sandbar at the mouth of the creek and no signs of a camp. The panthers continued straight toward us. I was sure that by now they had seen or scented us. Mary stopped praying. She took up one of the pistols. I told her that we could not shoot at them, even if they attacked us. The panthers swam on.

I imagined that they would swim past, perhaps on their way to some island in the swamp where they could rest safe from the dogs. But they came on. Then they were only a few feet away, and I feared they might try to climb into the boat. I held the rifle by the barrel, intending to use it as a club. They reached us, now so close that I could have touched the head of one of them with the rifle. It did not seem to me that they were even real. It was as if they had dropped down out of the sky, magical vaporous animals who would at any instant dissolve before our eyes like morning mist on the river touched by the rising sun. But I could see the track they had made through the duckweed. I knew that they were real.

They climbed out of the water onto one of the buttresses. They were sleek and grey, looking even thinner in their wet coats. They shook themselves, and the water sprayed over us. I smelled their stink. Then with effortless bounds they went up into the hollow cypress, their claws scratching against the bark.

Once they were inside it, it was as if they had never existed. But I could see the wet spots on the trunk and white places where their claws had torn through the bark and exposed the heart of the tree.

She asked me if they would disturb the child.

I told her they were not carrion eaters. And it was not likely they would even know the child was there behind the wall of mud. As I poled the boat away from the tree, we heard no more sounds from the dogs or the men. I hoped they had given up the chase. The panthers would rest in the hollow tree and then, perhaps in the early morning hours, swim for dry land.

I set a compass course and took us out of the swamp. We moved slowly and carefully. I tried not to make a sound as in the near darkness I poled the boat through the patches of duckweed. We went into the creek. I stopped the boat from time to time and listened for any sounds of the hunters or the smell of their fire. As Mary sat in the bow with both pistols in her lap, I took us out onto the river.

All night we traveled down the river and never saw a sign of the hunters. Neither of us spoke of the child. But I thought of the child. At least he would never be a slave. From time to time I had imagined him growing up in Haiti where I would have taught him to ride and shoot. It seemed to me that the world was darker and more horrible than I could have ever imagined. Nothing in the books I had read had prepared me for what I had experienced. I resolved to absolutely refuse to give myself up to despair, to keep the idea of a white house on a green hill overlooking the blue sea constantly in my mind. Mary and I would have children. We would be happy. A time would come when we would forget that terrible time on the river.

But my vision of the future melted away before my eyes when I looked at Mary who sat in the bow and wept. Sometimes I wondered whether that patch of darkness in the bow was Mary at all. I kept expecting her to throw herself over the side, and I was not sure if I would go in after her.

At first light I ran the boat up into a creek and found a thicket of willows. We plastered ourselves with mud and lay down to sleep as best we could as the coolness of the morning disappeared, and the heat lay heavy upon us.

"DOES HE HAVE IT all by heart?" Mason asked.

For some reason Mason found Paul's performance more disturbing than his claims about his experience at the bottom of the river with the turtle.

"Mostly," Robert said. "He got a few things turned around. But maybe his version is better than mine."

Paul picked up Octavius' manuscript. "I'm going to learn all of it."

"But why would you want to?" Henry asked.

Paul thought for a few moments. He turned to Robert. "Octavius spoke to me. He wants his words to appear through me. He wants me to be his instrument."

Mason let out a laugh, which he immediately suppressed.

Robert looked down at the sand. It did not seem possible that he had heard such a thing amid all the light of the morning, under that cloudless blue sky. Around a campfire he might have consented to at least playfully entertain such a possibility, but here, standing on the white sand, he listened to Paul's words fall and shatter against the light.

When Robert looked up again, he noticed Henry was staring off toward the river. Mason had developed a sudden interest in a piece of mussel shell.

"Let's go down the river," Henry said.

"Get some rest today, Paul," Mason said. "You've got to keep up with Robert's translating. Next thing you know, you'll be memorizing the encyclopedia."

Paul smiled, "I don't need to do that."

They broke camp and loaded the boats. While Robert and Henry lashed the side of one of the canopies to its frame. Mason was studying his maps. Paul was at the upstream end of the sandbar, sitting on the sand before Hoffman, who sat on his perch.

Mason packed up the maps and then walked up the sandbar to Paul. He stood next to Paul, who did not acknowledge his arrival in any way. Even Hoffman did not puff up his feathers or clack his beak. The bird cocked his head to one side and Mason looked into the single dark eye that was regarding him.

"Your bird has never taken to me," Mason said.

"He knows you shot him," Paul said. "What do you expect?"

"Now that makes good sense. There ain't nothing wrong with you."

"Octavius spoke to me."

"You mean when you read his words."

Paul stood up. "No, he spoke."

"That's making me nervous."

Paul wondered if Mason thought he had been speaking to the devil. Octavius' voice had been clear and distinct, repeating the words of the narrative as Paul said them. And sometimes saying other things as if they were two parts of a chorus in a Greek play.

"Then don't believe it," Paul said.

"Then where is he? Is he like a ghost? Does he only come out at night?"

"What do you want from me?"

"I want to know."

"All right. I'll show you. See, he's there and there and there." Mason began to walk up and down before Hoffman and point his finger in all directions. "Don't you see him standing there in the middle of the river? Don't you see him walking on water? That's something you can understand, Mason. You believe in the Bible. There're things stranger than what I'm telling you in the Bible.

Believe what I say. And he's coming. He's going to stick that Bowie knife of his in your heart."

Mason turned and walked away without another word. And he thought to himself that Paul was right. He had considered whether Paul had gotten himself mixed up with the devil. Now it seemed likely that might be true.

Robert and Henry had watched the encounter between the two take place.

"I wonder what that was all about?" Henry asked.

"I think that Paul's talk of ghosts is making Mason nervous," Robert said.

"I expect it would."

"But not you?"

"Not me. And you?"

"Maybe I'd like to but I can't."

Robert thought of Elaine, how she had died in a place where ghosts were part of the landscape, like the trees, the birds, and the chimpanzees. Some there might think her ghost had remained behind when he took her body home. After all, she loved those mountains.

Mason was walking toward them at a leisurely pace. He stopped and looked back at Paul.

"If we had Octavius here, what would you say to him?" Robert asked Henry.

"What do you mean?"

"Should he continue what he's doing?"

"I think he should love that woman. That's his only chance."

"At what?"

"At having his life mean anything at all We know what's going to happen to him. He made it to Haiti, but he wasn't satisfied. So he returned to Mississippi and bought the house and went to Paris and died."

Mason walked up to them. "Let's get ole crazy Paul and the buzzard into a boat and get on down the river."

Once they were underway Paul lay down amidships beneath

the canopy and went to sleep. Hoffman sat motionless on his perch beside him. Robert worked on the next chapter, wondering as Paul slept if he were dreaming of Octavius.

Chapter Thirteen

THE RIVER WIDENED and deepened; they made excellent time. Mason studied the map and predicted they were two days away from Columbia. They saw no game. But when they stopped at noon at a sandbar, Mason filled his net on the first cast with bream and crappie. They ate fish and grits. Robert and Henry lay down under the tarp and went to sleep.

Paul and Mason were occupied with plastering themselves with mud and letting it bake in the sun. Hoffman sat on his perch beneath the tarp and watched them.

"I like this better than repellent," Mason said. "That stuff makes me itch. Inside this mud I feel just like an apple pie."

"If we had feathers it'd be even better," Paul said. "But I guess mosquitoes can get at Hoffman on his neck."

"Now, don't start getting weird again. I don't like mosquitoes but I ain't planning to turn myself into a buzzard."

"I was never weird."

"You was dancing with the devil."

Paul picked up the manuscript and walked off to the tarp. Mason followed him. Paul sat down beside the bird. Mason watched his lips moving as he practiced what he had memorized.

"You don't have to get mad," Mason said. "I'm just telling you the truth."

Paul held up his hand for Mason to be quiet.

"All right, all right. Books and words is all you school teachers think about."

Mason lay down under the tarp. He listened to the sound of Paul's voice as he recited the Octavius' story. Paul was speaking softly. Every now and then Mason could make out a word or a piece of a phrase. As he drifted off to sleep, he smelled the scent of the dried mud on his body. It smelt of decay and a little of fish.

OUT ON THE river again, Robert worked on the translation beneath the canopy.

All afternoon they pushed hard, resting only occasionally in the shade to refill the gas tanks. They were beginning to run low on fuel, but Mason had calculated they had enough to reach Columbia.

"The next stop's Bougalosa," Robert said. "We'll refuel there. That should get us to the Gulf."

"We'll smell our way to Bougalosa," Henry said.

"Smell what?" Robert asked.

"The paper mill. It'll be like we were sailing right into the mouth of Hell," said Henry.

Mason handed one of his maps to Paul along with a marking pencil. "Show us where the devil lives?"

"Inside of us," Paul replied. "Haven't you been paying attention to Ocatavius' story?"

It seemed to Robert that this was a good sign that Paul could make a joke about the encounter he claimed to have had with Octavius. But perhaps this was not a joke, perhaps he was serious.

"There's no devil in me," Mason said. "I've been saved. Happened when I was twelve years old."

"That the first time you handled snakes?" Henry asked. "Were you the one who took 'em out of the box and threw 'em into the crowd?"

"You're the one who handles snakes," Mason replied. "We've all seen you do it."

Henry laughed. "And so I have. But I believe if one bites me

I'll get sick."

"God even watches over school teachers," Mason said.

Paul handed the map to Mason. "That's where Hell is."

Mason took a look at the map and began to laugh. He held it up for Henry and Robert to see. Paul had filled the path of the river with Xs.

"Boys, this ain't the Pearl, it's that River Styx, the one in the fairy tale books. It ain't never gonna end. Yell out real loud if you see the devil."

WHEN THE SUN hung just above the tops of the trees, they cut the motors and placed a rifleman in the bow of each boat. Although there were a few bluffs, mostly it was cypress swamp on either side. But no deer appeared. Doves flew in to the sandbars, whistling overhead and then dropping down to drink, flashes of grey against the white sand. Robert was considering taking a stand and shooting enough for supper when Henry shot a doe as she came down to drink at a sandbar.

They butchered the deer and ate their fill. Paul ate quickly and went off to memorize the new chapter. He walked back and forth just outside the circle of firelight. The men could hear the sound of his words but seldom make out the sense. He could not understand why he was having so much trouble remembering the words. What was easy before now seemed impossibly difficult. It was as if the words were scrambling themselves, their individual syllables and consonants forming themselves into unintelligible combinations.

"I wonder why this one's giving him trouble?" Henry said. "I thought he had it just as fast as he could read it."

"Maybe he don't like what he's reading," said Mason.

"Paul, are you ready?" Robert called.

Paul appeared in the circle of firelight and shook his head. Then he disappeared into the darkness again and resumed his roaming about the fire. He found himself no longer even trying to understand the words and gave himself up to the sounds, pure sound that ultimately yielded no sense at all. Finally they all gave up on him and went to sleep.

THEY ATE VENISON for breakfast. Henry had stayed up tending the meat. He awakened them by banging a pole against the side of a boat. He had already made coffee.

"It took all night but I've got it," Paul said.

A few hours before sunrise those chaotic syllables and consonants which he had been chanting for hours, coalesced into meaning. He had sat on the sand and cried, thankful that he was not going to be condemned to madness.

After they ate, Paul stood before them, Hoffman on a perch at his feet, and began to recite the chapter as they lounged about under the tarp. Robert held the manuscript and followed it as Paul talked.

Love

Mary moved as if she were in a dream. She talked and ate and smeared mud on her body against the mosquitoes, but it was as if she heard nothing I said to her. She would not talk of the child at all.

We saw no sign of other people on the river, which unrolled before us every night, no light from a fire or a lantern, no smell of smoke, and no shouts or clear notes from a hunter's horn or gunshots. It was as no one existed in the entire territory of Mississippi except us. Once during the day, as we lay in the mouth of a creek, slipping in and out of a sleep made difficult by the heat and the mosquitoes, I heard someone pass on the river. They were singing, and there was the splash of paddles. I sat up quickly with the rifle in my hands, almost tipping the pirogue over. She put her hands on my shoulders and told me that it was a dream, that I was dreaming. She took the rifle out of my hands and laid it back down in the pirogue. The mosquitoes hummed about my ears as I lay down, the wet wood cool against by body. I took slow deep breaths to calm myself.

I shot a deer, and we spent a night smoking the meat. I had decided that there was less chance of someone on the river seeing our fire, which we built on a sandbar down in the creek channel, than there was of someone spotting the smoke. When we went back out onto the river at night, I wished that the night would last forever. I wanted to run down river until we reached the sea, until I could smell the salt in the air. I imagined how it would be to arrive at the river's mouth at dawn one morning and see the Gulf stretching out flat and blue and endless.

I did not want to have to kill another man, but I knew it was likely I would. And I wondered if Strode Maury had taught me this at the same time he taught me of love between men, showing me what to do with my body, and at the same time he had taught me this other thing, and I had not known I had learned it at all.

I required a boat capable of sailing to Haiti. It needed to be small enough for one man to handle. A whale boat with a sail would be enough. But someone would have possession of that boat, and if it were in use or guarded I would have to kill to take it. And then we could no longer travel under the cover of darkness. But the Gulf was an enormous place, and there would be no reason for anyone to investigate a small boat. If we were lucky, no one would even see us. We would see a ship before they saw us, and I could lower the sail and hope we would be concealed by the swells.

Toward morning the wind rose; the sky to the west was lit with flashes of lightning. I busied myself packing the meat away. When the rain came, we would huddle together under a piece of canvas. At least the rain would make the morning cool. We were both covered with sweat from tending the fire on the hot night. We were naked and plastered with mud against the mosquitoes. I welcomed the thought of the rain washing me clean and cooling my body.

The velocity of the wind continued to rise. The wind picked up the embers from the fire and scattered them about the creek bank where they glowed for a moment before disappearing. The thunder boomed and the lightning flashed. Mary was frightened and put her arms around me. She was singing that low song of hers, the one she sang when the baby died.

The wind increased, bending the willows flat against the ground and tearing from the treetops leaves and small branches, which fell like a rain upon us. In a lightning flash I saw a large white bird come hurtling over us, only a few feet above our heads. It fell onto the opposite bank with a thud. In the next flash I saw that its neck was broken. It lay there in the mud looking as if someone had wadded up one of Strode Maury's fine linen shirts and tossed it across the creek.

Now the sound came, a heavy sound I could liken only to a locomotive. And I knew of that only from one experience, when Strode Maury took me with him to Atlanta as his body servant. We rode on a train together. At the hotel the other men's servants slept on pallets on the floor beside their masters, but I slept in the bed with him. That was my first year with him. He had bought me in Charleston. And in the morning we had coffee and ham and eggs in bed together. It was the best ham I had ever tasted.

I knew the sound was a whirlwind. One had passed through Strode Maury's plantation a year before and had cut a neat path through the timber. Trees were snapped and broken. It was as if a man had cut a path through a cotton field with a cane, leaving tramped and mangled plants in his wake. One morning Strode Maury, as I watched, shot a deer in the tangle as the buck walked out to feed on the tender plants that had sprung up in the newly created open space.

The sound came on toward us, heavy and huge. Still not a drop of rain had fallen. I pushed Mary down into the bottom of the pirogue and lay on top of her. Then it was on us and the wind howled. A whirlwind formed between the banks of the creek. The pirogue, caught in it, spun in a circle. Mary was screaming. I imagined us being borne aloft, our bodies torn into pieces by the force of the wind. A tree came down with a crash, the tips of its upper branches falling across my back. Then the wind was gone. I heard the enormous, heavy sound of the whirlwind moving off to the northeast. I pitied any living thing that fell in its path.

The rain came, large heavy drops. I had never experienced such a rain. It scoured the mud from our bodies and ripped more leaves from the canopy above us. It filled the pirogue with water.

Then as suddenly as it began, it stopped. We stood naked and shivering in the sudden coolness. Water dripped on us from the leaves above. Behind the clouds the sun was rising, the light leaking through, and illuminating the destruction left by the whirlwind. A jumble of snapped-off tree trunks a few yards up the creek marked the place where the whirlwind had crossed.

She was crying, and I took her in my arms to warm and comfort her. She spoke the name of the child over and over and asked me if I thought the whirlwind would uproot the big cypress. I told her it would not come close to the cypress. She said she could not endure the thought of the child's body being eaten by animals. I told her that the burial was safe, that it would endure for hundreds of years like the mummified bodies of Egyptian kings. It was likely that no man had ever ventured into the swamp until we had, and it was likely that no man ever would.

I felt myself hard against her. I had never had a woman. The only thing I knew of love was Strode Maury, spreading me in his insistent way.

She lay down in the pirogue and looked up at me. Overhead the birds were singing wildly. The air was cool and damp. A breeze came up and I shivered. She told me she would make me warm, that we would make each other warm.

She raised her legs and hooked them over the sides of the pirogue. She guided me into her. I was clumsy and awkward, but she stroked my back and set the rhythm. Then at some point the rhythm became mine and then became ours, both of us moving together. The songs of the birds were in my ears until our cries shattered those sweet songs.

Afterwards she told me that although we had been killing people ever since she met me, that now we had made a life instead of taking one. And I wondered if she truly knew if we had made a child. I imagined what it would be like to watch her grow big and then the birth, not on some river sandbar, but in a great house with paintings on the walls and silk curtains hanging from the windows and outside a view of the blue Caribbean Sea. I had imagined that house many times. I had planned on building it when I reached Haiti, but now for the first time I could imagine filling it with people: my wife, our children.

The sun came out and the coolness quickly was driven away. The mosquitoes flew in swarms about us again. We swam in the creek and ate some venison. Then we plastered mud on each other and lay down in the pirogue to sleep and wait for darkness.

As we lay in that hot stillness, Mary told me how she ran away. At the end of the work day, she had slipped away in the dusk as the overseer was escorting the workers back to their cabins. Already she knew she was with child. She had decided that she would not allow the child to be born into slavery.

She had no plan, no final object other than freedom. She told me that she had a vague idea of living with the child in the great pine forest. She ate berries and turtles and insects, anything she could catch or gather with her hands. Then the charcoal burner found her.

I imagined her wandering through the forest. She was lucky that she had not been eaten by a panther, and I told her so. She raised her head and looked at me. I could see her two dark eyes staring out of the mask of grey mud. She told me that she was not afraid to die, that freedom was more important than living. And she told me that all that time she was in the forest she was never afraid. It was easy to find food with her hands, just as long as she was willing to eat anything. But the insects had tormented her, and she wished that she had known about the mud. She only became afraid when the charcoal burner discovered her. She had realized that he was going to take her back for the reward. She had planned to kill him after he helped her with the birth of the child.

I asked her what she had planned to do when winter came on. She was moving north. I told her that the farther she moved north the colder it would become. She said that it was impossible to move south, for she had no knowledge of sailing.

I tried to imagine how it was for her. To the north stretched swamps and the pine forest, to the south was the Gulf, and I was certain she had no conception of it at all, only that it was immense.

And then I asked her if she knew the father of the child. She told me that it was a young field hand who worked in the same gang as she. He had cut himself with an ax and his blood had become poisoned and he had died. She was crying now, the tears making dark tracks on her cheeks. I told her that I was sorry. She said that it did not matter, that he would have been sold or she and the child would have been sold. They were all doomed.

I told her that I had no idea of my parents. I could only recall a woman, not my mother, who took care of me. She worked as a cook in the big house. I had plenty to eat and cast-off clothes to wear. I was training to become a house servant. But the master died and we were all sold. Strode Maury bought me.

I had no intention of telling her what passed between Strode Maury and me. And my desire was for her, not for a man. I wondered how it would have been between Strode Maury and the woman who was coming from New Orleans. She would have been a thing of expediency for him, but to hold her he would have had to bed her. He needed her; he needed children. And I wondered if he could have gone from me to the woman without a thought.

We both went to sleep. I woke at mid-afternoon to her hands on me. We both ignored the mosquitoes and satiated ourselves. Afterwards we swam and replastered ourselves with mud and ate more venison. Then we slept again.

At dusk I poled the boat out of the creek and onto the river. The storm had moved through too quickly to affect the water level. Somewhere, very far off, I thought I heard a sound. I took the pole out of the water and told Mary to listen. But as we sat there beneath the dark sky full of stars, both listening intently, it never came again. There were only the familiar sounds of the insects and frogs and the calls of night birds. I took up the pole and threw my weight against it, the

*pirogue shooting forward through the darkness
toward the Gulf.*

PAUL PUT HOFFMAN on his arm and walked out from beneath the
tarp and across the sand, headed up river. He needed to be alone
for a while. He felt an urgent desire to repeat what he had just
recited again and again. And he feared that if he did not calm himself, he would become like a digital track someone had programmed
to play itself over and over.

"Not as good this time," Robert said. "But he got most of it."

"Octavius will never get away from Strode Maury," Henry said.
"He thinks it'll be easy, but it won't."

Henry knew he had not been able to escape from the legacy
of slavery even through he was separated from it by several gen-
erations. It influenced the way he looked at everything. He supposed that was why the science of grass was so attractive. That
legacy could not influence the way he looked at a species of grass.
The scientific method provided him with an immutable way to
look.

"I wonder what would have happened if he'd stayed with ole
Strode," Mason said. "What would have happened if that woman
had figured it out."

Robert thought of the young woman, used to the rich life in
New Orleans, coming to the isolation and tedium of the plantation. "She would have gone home to New Orleans. If she could
have believed it. Which I doubt."

"I think she'd have figured it out," Henry said. She'd have
watched the way he looked at Octavius. She'd have known."

"Girls didn't know things like that then," said Mason.

"She would've known," Henry said. "Even if she couldn't say
what she was feeling. She'd have felt it and that would've been
enough. And like I said, Octavius was doomed no matter what he
did. If that woman had come up from New Orleans, she'd have
been doomed too."

"Look at him," Mason said.

They all turned their attention to Paul who, hatless, was standing as still as a wading bird at the end of the sandbar in one of his reveries. Hoffman, who sat on his arm, had his head cocked to one side and was staring at him.

"One day he's gonna cook his brains," Mason said. "I wouldn't want that buzzard looking at me like that."

They all agreed they would try to persuade him to leave when they reached Columbia.

"A few days with Elizabeth and he'll be fine," said Robert. But he wondered as he said it if that would really be the case.

Henry poured himself another cup of coffee. "Maybe we should all go home at Columbia?"

"Anyone who wants to should," Robert said. "I'm going to the Gulf."

Everyone except Henry agreed they would continue the journey.

Henry poured what remained of his cup of coffee onto the sand. "Tastes like I used river water to make it. I guess I'll stick it out. We should be able to run under power. We'll make good time."

They loaded the boats. When they left, Paul was still standing motionless on the sand. Mason brought the boat in to him.

"Come on, Paul," Mason said. "Let's go down the river."

Paul looked up, as if he were surprised that the boat was there, and stepping into it took a seat in the bow. Mason persuaded him to come under the canopy. Paul put Hoffman on his perch. Mason started the motor and the boats moved off down river on parallel tracks. Robert sat in the bow with the manuscript, enjoying the breeze in his face. He watched the forested banks unroll on either side for a few minutes before he turned his attention to the words of Octavius.

Chapter Fourteen

THEY RAN ALL morning under power. When they came to a place where three pipelines passed over the river in succession, Mason, who held the map in his hand, pointed out that they were not far from Columbia. It might be possible to reach it before nightfall.

At noon they halted on a sandbar for lunch. The river was wider than usual and deeper. Someone had a trotline set out, marked by plastic milk jugs which served as floats. While they ate, Paul went to the foot of the sandbar and stood motionless in a reverie. Hoffman sat on a perch beside him. They called to him, but he ignored them.

Paul found himself caught in the narrative, which he was silently reciting from the beginning. This time the words were all in place in his head. They came easily and effortlessly to him, but he paid no attention to their meaning. He was counting the syllables.

Henry walked down to him. He could see Paul's lips moving. Hoffman was watching him.

"Paul," Henry said.

Paul held up his hand for silence and turned his head away from Henry. Henry stepped close to Paul and put his hand on his shoulder. "Come and eat." Paul was trembling. "It's all right."

Paul had lost the count and knew it would be impossible now to take it up again.

"I'm all right," Paul said.

"You sure?"

"Yes."

"Let's go eat."

Henry put his hand around Paul's shoulder. Paul was no longer trembling. He took up Hoffman on his arm. Together he and Henry walked back to the tarp.

They came under the tarp and Paul put Hoffman on his perch. Paul took up a plastic water bottle and drained what remained in it in one long swallow.

"I think we should buy some cold beer in Columbia," Paul said.

"That's the smartest thing I've heard anyone say today," said Mason.

Robert and Henry agreed that it was a good idea.

Robert hoped that Paul would turn his attention to the banality of daily existence, to things like cold beer. Perhaps he was going to break free of his obsession with the manuscript. They could all go on to the Gulf together.

Paul ate some deer jerky, which he shared with Hoffman. He and Hoffman had a drink of water. Mason had had no luck with his cast net. The lines they had set out had yielded nothing. Mason had even gone out and run the trot line, but the hooks were all empty.

"Let's go shoot some fish," Mason said to Robert.

"Where?" Robert asked.

"That creek we passed. That'll be a good place. It'll be cool up in there."

So Robert agreed to go with him, more for the coolness than the fish. The others were not interested in shooting fish.

They took the boat back upriver to the mouth of the creek, which was only a few hundred yards away. A sandbar blocked the mouth. They left the boat there and waded into the green tunnel.

It was cool, just as Robert had hoped it would be. The water was shallow and a yellowish color but clear, like whiskey, and seldom deeper than their knees. Schools of minnows fled at their approach; small water snakes dropped off of overhanging willow branches and swam away, scoring the water with their smooth curves.

"Nothing in here," Robert said.

He carried the bow with a barbed fish arrow across the string.

The image of the rain forest and Elaine's blue backpack suddenly appeared in his mind, like a fish rising from the bottom of a deep pool. He supposed it was all the green that had triggered it. And he imagined himself hunting the poachers with the bow, with poisoned arrows. He hit a muddy place in the sandy bottom and stumbled.

"Be quiet," Mason said. "You'll spook the fish."

Robert was still in the rain forest, peering into the green to try to find something that looked like a piece of a human figure.

Mason looked down at the water, holding his shotgun at port arms.

"What you shooting?"

"Number two buckshot."

"Won't be any fish left."

"Quiet!"

So they walked in silence in parallel tracks up the creek. He heard the chatter of a kingfisher. Ahead, hidden by a bend, something dropped into the creek, making a solid splash. A mosquito buzzed in his ear. He looked at Mason, who moved slowly, careful not to make splashes and disturb the fish.

He was sifting through his mind, searching for that image of the rain forest again (he thought that if he had not been interrupted that he might have seen the face of one of the poachers), when the shotgun went off, the sound amplifying between the narrow banks of the creek. Mason shot again, pumping the gun, the water torn by the buckshot. He was shooting fast, swinging the gun as he would on a bird, and tracking something across the water. Then the gun was empty. Two large bass floated to the top, one minus most of its head, the other hardly marked at all.

"I told you there were fish in this creek," Mason said. "You'd been paying attention we could've got the other one."

"Octavius didn't shoot fish," Robert observed. "Couldn't afford to waste the shot and powder."

"My daddy showed me how to do this." Mason turned and looked out the green tunnel of the creek at the brightness of the river. "I wish we never had to get off this river. But we will. You'll go to Haiti. I'll go back to drinking up Mama's check."

"You'll enroll again at the community college. Get a job at a golf club."

"Maybe."

Mason was still looking intently at the river. Robert heard the staccato call of a pileated woodpecker from deep in the woods.

"I'd be all right if I could just stay on this river," Mason said. "Forever."

"I'm thinking about buying a boat and going on to Haiti," Robert said. "You could come with me."

"We'll come home. You'll go back to translating and I'll go back to the running after women at them clubs."

Mason handed Robert the shotgun. Mason was thinking of abandoning the golf course idea. He wanted to find out how you became a mapmaker. He planned on asking Henry about that. Mason took up one fish in either hand. He started toward the river and Robert followed.

When they reached the camp, they found the others standing at the foot of the sandbar, looking at the deep pool that lay past it. Hoffman sat on his perch under the tarp. Robert and Mason walked down to join them.

Paul pointed at the pool. "There's a big gar out there. It's enormous. I'll bet it's longer than one of the boats."

They all looked at the pool, the sun's glare cut by their polarized glasses. No one saw any sign of a fish like that.

"Did you see it, Henry?" Robert asked, thinking as he continued to look at the pool that neither it nor the river seemed big enough to hold a fish like that.

"No, I was asleep. I heard something in the pool. It sounded like someone had tossed a cinder block into it. Paul told me it was that big fish."

"Bigger than the one at the state museum in Jackson?" Mason asked.

"Yes," Paul said.

"How big is that one?" Robert asked.

"An alligator gar fifteen feet long," Henry said.

"Say the name for us, Henry," said Mason.

"*Lepisosteus spatula*. A man could put his head in the mouth of the one at the museum. My cousin took me to see it. He told me fish like that lived in the creek where we swam. I'd imagine one of them swallowing me in one bite. I had nightmares about that thing."

"Let's catch it," Mason said. "It's not worth eating. But we can give it to the museum. It'll have our names on it. Scare little children after we're dead and gone."

Robert could easily imagine the gar had been some sort of hallucination for Paul, a waking daydream just like the voice of Octavius. "I don't see how something that big could be in this river," he said.

They all walked back up to the tarp. Mason began to prepare the bass he had shot. They could all clearly see the pool from where they were sitting. It was perfectly still, looking like a piece of polished black glass. Hoffman followed the gaze of the men and began to look in the direction of the pool.

"Hoffman knows it's there," Paul said.

Henry started to say something but was interrupted by Mason. "My lines."

The float he had set out was moving upstream. Then it went under. Mason ran across the sand and pulled it in. He had caught a good-sized catfish.

Mason gutted the fish.

"Let me have those guts and head," Paul said. "I'll show you that gar."

Paul tied the guts to a cord float, once a piece of a seine. It still had a few patches of red paint on it. He threw the float out into the current so it would drift down to the pool.

They all watched it come to rest in the center of the pool. Nothing disturbed it.

"I guess that monster ain't hungry," Mason said.

"It's there," Paul said in a soft voice. "It's there."

But Robert had his doubts and so did Henry, who was trying to come up with other explanations for the large splash he had heard.

But as they were eating the bass, they all saw the huge head of the gar rise out of the dark water. Water sprayed; teeth flashed in the sun. It was as if some creature from the reign of dinosaurs had suddenly appeared before them. Then it was gone, disappearing with a swirl under the water. The float had vanished.

"God, he's right!" Mason said. "Did you see that thing?"

Everyone agreed the fish was as big as Paul had claimed.

They held a discussion about the best method for catching the gar. Mason was for using dynamite, his usual solution, but all of them were against that.

"Mason can swim down and tie a rope to its tail," Henry said.

"I'm not getting in the water with that thing. I may never swim in the river again." Instead, Mason suggested that they lure it to the surface again and shoot it with one of the rifles. But no one else wanted to do that.

"We can't shoot it or explode it," Robert said. "It's just not right to kill it that way."

"How old can one of those fish get?" Mason asked Henry.

"Not as old as a turtle," Henry said.

"It's too big for this river," said Paul. "Henry, do you think it was here when Octavius passed through? Do you think it's been living right here ever since then?"

"No," Henry said. "It's just a big fish."

"I know how we can kill it," said Paul.

"Well, I'm glad to hear that," Henry said. "Mason went down and put a rope around that big turtle's tail. That's what got that turtle out of the river. Those turtle steaks were mighty good. I remember you ate a few of them. Just what have you got in mind for that fish?"

"We'll harpoon it."

"I don't recall us bringing along a harpoon," Henry said.

"We'll make one. Out of Robert's arrows."

Robert shook his head. "It'll never work."

"We could bundle them together," Henry said.

And then everyone had ideas. Mason and Paul went into the woods to cut poplar shafts for a harpoon and lances while Henry and Robert broke out Robert's barbed fish arrows.

They lashed three of arrows together with nylon cord and left a loop in the cord to attach a strong line. The problem of making a socket for the shaft so that it would separate from the bundle of arrows after someone plunged the arrows into the gar was more difficult. Henry cut a piece of aluminum tubing off the canopy with a hacksaw from the tool kit and slipped it over the end of the shaft. Then he forced the bundle of arrows into the shaft. It was securely attached so that all the force of a throw would be transferred into the head of the harpoon, but it would also cleanly separate when the fish was struck.

Mason went out and took the milk jugs from the trot line. These they tied to the line as floats, so that they would mark the passage of the fish and provide extra drag against which it would have to fight.

They lashed two machetes to the poles. They would kill the fish with these once they had used the harpoon and line to bring it to the surface.

"Now who's going to do it?" Robert asked.

Everyone wanted to be the one to strike the fish.

"I'm the one," Paul said.

"I think Robert should do it," Henry said. "He's got the strongest arm. Think about that serve of yours, Paul. That harpoon has got to penetrate those scales and go deep enough so it'll hold."

But Paul refused to concede and Mason was arguing too.

"We'll cut cards," Robert said. "Then everybody gets one chance in the order of the cut."

Mason got out the cards and they all drew. Robert drew a deuce, Mason a ten, Henry a nine, and Paul, who drew last, held out an ace for all of them to see.

"It was meant to be," Paul said.

"You sure you want to kill that fish?" Henry asked. "We don't want somebody throwing that harpoon who's got his mind half made up."

"I have to kill it," said Paul.

"I can't listen to anymore of this," Henry said. "Let's do it."

It took Mason a long time to catch another catfish. They all lay beneath the tarp and watched his lines. No one talked of the fish. Instead they spoke of their progress down the river and of the cold beer they planned to buy in Columbia. When after a time no fish took the bait, they, by unspoken agreement, stopped watching the floats, leaving that job to Mason.

PAUL SOON LEFT the tarp and went to the edge of the pool and stood gazing out into the water. It seemed to him that the discovery of the big fish had returned him to a sort of clarity. It was as if he were looking at the trees, the sky, and the river for the first time. He hoped that at the moment he drove the harpoon into it he would be treated to some sort of revelation. He imagined standing there in the boat while a rain of baby turtles softly fell from the sky and dimpled the smooth surface of the pool.

Mason joined him.

"Why do you want to kill that fish?" Mason asked. "Octavius tell you to do that?"

"He no longer speaks to me," Paul said.

Mason looked out at the pool. The whole affair of the fish had unsettled him in some way he could not precisely define. "You don't think Octavius is in that fish?"

"Is the Jonah story your favorite in the Bible?"

"I just want to know what you're thinking."

Paul sat on the sand and put his feet in the water. Mason sat down beside him.

"I'm thinking that I can see just as well as Hoffman."

They both turned and looked at Hoffman who was sitting on his perch under the tarp looking at them.

Mason picked up a mussel shell and skipped it across the pool. One, two, three times it bounced and then sank out of sight. "Can you see that shell lying on the bottom?"

"No."

"Can you see the fish?"

"No."

"You can't. Your buzzard can't."

Robert wondered out loud what he and Paul were talking about.

"He probably thinks Octavius caught that fish when he passed by here and threw it back because it was too little," Henry said.

"My lines," Mason said.

Mason was up and running across the sand. He pulled another catfish out of the water. After he gutted and beheaded it, he walked to a boat and put the fish in the live well. Then he returned to the water's edge and held the head and guts up for them to see.

"Let's go!" he shouted. "Paul, you come take your turn."

PAUL CAREFULLY COILED the rope on the deck amidships behind the middle seat. Henry had cut a section off an eight-inch-thick poplar and lashed it upright in a frame of hickory poles he set between the front and middle seats. He took a turn in the line around the post. Henry and Mason, both wearing gloves, were to feed line to the fish, the post acting as a drag. Paul took the harpoon in his hands and stood on the seat. Mason paddled the boat out into the river. It was too deep to pole. Robert followed in the other boat.

When they reached the center of the river, Mason threw out the head and guts, to which he had attached a piece of float. The hunters drifted along, keeping the lure between the boats, Paul poised in the bow with the harpoon. Everyone watched the water for any sign of the fish.

Robert peered into the dark water. His glasses cut the glare, but he could see only a few schools of minnows. A turtle swam close to the surface and then dived out of sight. The head and guts floated amid a greasy slick; the sun was suspended in the water as a pale yellow ball. They all waited. No one spoke or moved.

"There," Henry said.

Paul turned to follow where Henry was pointing. The fish swam toward the boat. Robert saw it clearly now. It was big and longer than the boats, and it rose in a leisurely fashion, its delicate, feathery-looking fins belying its enormous size. It looked as if it were flying through the water. Paul raised the harpoon above his head. Now the fish was coming up, its jaws open wide as it closed in on the entrails, rising fast now. And Robert thought that one of its eyes was looking straight at him. The fish struck the bait, its jaws closing with a popping sound. As it started to dive, its back rose clear of water. Paul gave out a yell as he released the harpoon, driving it into a point just behind the ventral fin.

The fish disappeared, and the line (with five empty milk jugs attached to the front end), passed hissing through the gloved hands of Henry and Mason. As the boat, towed by the fish, shot off downriver, the rope continued to pay out and passed smoking around the post. Mason dipped water out of the river with a cup and threw it on the post to cool it.

Robert followed in his boat. By the time he reached it they were a quarter of a mile down the river. Most of the line had been paid out. Mason made an extra wrap of it around the post and tied it off. The fish had stopped at the bottom of a deep pool.

"Already tired out," Mason said. "A gar don't have much staying power."

"He's so big, he doesn't need staying power," Robert said. "Why, that fish could tow us to the Gulf."

"He won't," Paul said. "He's lying down there at the bottom of that pool. He'll stay there."

Robert followed the line down into the pool. The rope, stretched tight, looked as if it were made of steel. Now that the fish was out of sight it was as if it did not exist at all. Yet there was the line. Robert maneuvered the boat over to it with a paddle (the river was far too deep at this point for poling) and put his hand on it. The line felt exactly as he had imagined, like a steel cable. The fish was like a deadman, buried deep beneath the bottom of the river, and there was no way they could ever move it.

"If that fish finds a deep enough hole and dives, it'll pull the boat under," Robert said.

"I hope he runs again," Mason said. "Let him pull us all the way to the Gulf. He'll have nothing left. Be out of gas."

Paul was taking off his clothes. Then he stood there in the bow, his hand on the rope. He took Mason's lance out of his hands.

"You be careful," Mason said. He grinned. "That thing could swallow you in one bite."

"I'm just going to tickle him," said Paul.

"Don't do it," Henry said.

Paul laughed and slipped over the side. He took a series of deep breaths and then disappeared, going down the rope toward the fish. All of them except Henry, who was looking at the second hand of his watch, gazed at the dark water.

"Thirty seconds," Henry said.

"Can he kill it?" Mason asked.

"No," said Robert. "But he can stir it up."

"That thing can take an arm or leg off with no trouble at all," Mason said.

"It won't happen to Paul," said Henry.

"If he's unlucky, it'll happen," Mason said.

Henry glanced down at his watch. "One minute."

Robert looked at the smooth, blank surface of the water. The rope had not changed its position.

Then the boat with Mason and Henry was gone. It shot off down river. Henry had his hands on the rope, and Mason was scrambling from the bow to reach him. Paul, gasping for air, shot to the surface beside Robert's boat, and climbed over the side. They went off in pursuit of the boat.

"Where'd you strike him?" Robert yelled to Paul.

"In the heart!" Paul shouted. "In the heart!"

But Paul had not struck the fish in the heart, for the fish ran longer this time, almost a mile. The river grew shallow again. Robert imagined that the fish was running for some deep pool, so deep that it would be beyond their reach.

The fish unexpectedly halted in a shallow place, where there was barely enough water to conceal it. Henry and Mason had gained back most of the line, which they had paid out as the fish had made its run. Now for the first time, Robert could see all of it. He watched its gills moving and saw where the harpoon was stuck in its back. Blood, creating a dark cloud in the clear water, flowed from its belly where Paul had made a slash with the lance. Its mouth gaped open, revealing rows of teeth.

Paul asked Henry for his lance, but Henry shook his head. "You had your chance."

Henry stood in the bow. Mason knelt beside him and using the line pulled the boat directly over the fish. Henry raised the lance and struck down just ahead of the ventral fin. The fish's back was only a foot beneath the water, so he was able to deliver the thrust with real force.

The fish in response turned back on itself and swam beneath Mason's boat. The boat tilted and then flipped over, spilling Mason, Paul, and Henry into the river. The boat, now turned sideways and kept on the surface by the flotation that had been installed under the seats, acted as a drag, but still the fish managed to tow it downriver for a hundred yards before stopping.

Robert took the others aboard the boat and moved slowly downstream. By the time they arrived the gar was floating belly up. It was a little longer than a boat.

"God, it'll be up on the wall in Jackson," Paul said. "Our names'll be there."

They righted the boat and spent some time retrieving the spilled gear, which was easy because of the shallow, clear water. Paul was able to start the motor. He had feared that being immersed had damaged it. He let it run at idle to dry it while they discussed the best way to transport the gar.

Mason studied his maps again. "We're only a couple of hours from Columbia."

"Not towing that thing," Henry said.

Mason agreed that he was right.

"We'll travel at night if we have to," Robert said. "That thing's going to rot and stink unless we get it into cold storage."

Paul was in the water with the fish, which lay with its mouth open. He ran his finger over a tooth. Robert stood beside him, but he did not touch the fish.

"Are you sorry we killed him?" Robert asked.

"No," Paul said. "I felt him down there. I couldn't see him, but I felt him. I could hear the sound of his heart beating."

"Well, it's not beating anymore," Mason said. "Get back in the boat and let's start the tow."

Robert reached out and put his hand on the fish. He ran his fingertips over the slick scales. He had been just as eager for the hunt as the others. He looked down the river. It would be different traveling it and knowing the fish was no longer there. It was unlikely others as large as it existed. He had had the same feeling once when he crossed a channelized section of the Tombigbee in northern Mississippi. The once twisting river ran perfectly straight between treeless banks and a barge, bound for Mobile, was moving down it. It was the same water but now devoid of interest if not of life, a chalk line-straight sterile channel unraveling before the eyes of the barge pilot.

"Come on," Mason said. "Let's go."

They got underway. It was late afternoon, and Robert knew that they would be half the night getting to Columbia. If they ran out of fuel, they would not get there at all. This was the first day since they started the journey he had not worked on the translation. He longed to be at the manuscript. But by the time they reached Columbia at least he would know what it felt to travel the river at night. Robert considered those water striders, who danced over still pools on the surface tension. What was beneath them they never knew. Although he could go down the river at night and read

Octavius' words, he could at best attain only a dim idea of what it felt like to travel in that pirogue, what it felt like to be hunted, the fear a constant thing like the smell of the mud and the hum of the insects.

Chapter Fifteen

THEY TIED A line to the fish's tail and began the tow. Robert had hoped they would be able to go at some reasonable speed, but the tow proceeded at a slow pace. He concluded they would be lucky if they reached Columbia before morning. Mason studied the maps and kept track of their progress. He estimated they had barely enough gas.

Henry disagreed. "We'll come up a little short."

"Maybe," Mason replied.

"It looks like a dragon," said Paul.

The fish lay half submerged, its scales glistening in the sunlight.

"Or a dead fish," Mason said.

Mason and Henry continued their argument about the gas. Paul joined in and sided with Mason.

As the sun was falling behind the trees, the motor on Paul's boat ran out of gas. The one on Robert's boat had already begun to sputter and cough. They poured what was left of the gas into the tanks. Mason made some quick calculations. He estimated that they were a couple of miles above Columbia. Henry suggested that when the gas ran low they transfer all the gas to one boat and have it make a run to the town to fill the tanks.

The rank stink of the gar filled the air.

"In a few hours it'll start to rot," Henry said. "We couldn't stand to be near it."

They moved down the river again. Gradually the light faded from the sky, and the evening star rose. Robert took a turn at the motor. Henry and Paul had moved up to the bow seats with a light to look out for snags. Then it was dark and all the stars were out. There was no moon. They ran down river through the dense, hot darkness, their lights probing the river ahead.

A mile or so above the first highway bridge that crossed the river above the town they stopped to transfer what was left of the gas to Mason's boat. As they were engaged they heard another boat coming up the river and then saw its light as it swung around a bend.

The boat stopped. A figure played a spotlight light over their boats and the fish. It was a bass boat. In the backwash from the light the boat sparkled from the glitter, like thousands of stars, embedded in its fiberglass hull.

"Hey, you out here spotlighting deer," Mason complained. "Get that light out of our eyes."

"Sorry about that," a voice said. The light settled back on the fish.

"You boys have caught a whale," a second voice said.

"If I'd of known that thing was in the river, I'd of sold my boat and taken up golf," the first voice said.

"Look, they got a pet buzzard," the second voice said.

The light played over Hoffman, who flapped his good wing and hissed.

"You've never seen a vulture before?" Paul asked.

"Why'd you want to cozy up to it?" the first voice said.

"I'd rather have a buzzard than a chicken," the second voice added.

"Well, I ain't against chickens," the first voice said. "Chickens bought this boat."

The light was turned toward the sky. The man in the bow used the electric trolling motor to bring the bass boat in between the John boats.

The man in the bow introduced himself as William Foster. The man in the stern was James Street. Questions were asked on both sides and before long everyone knew where everyone else was from. William and James worked at a chicken plant. They had come straight from their jobs to fish all night on the river.

"How'd yawl catch that thing?" William asked.

Henry explained about Paul's work with the harpoon. He handed it to the men to examine.

James pulled the head out of the socket and turned it over in his hands. "I wish I'd been there to see that." He handed it to William.

William ran his finger over the edge of one of the broad heads. "It must have been something. You stuck him good with this."

"That fish is going to the state museum in Jackson," Paul said.

"All our names will be on it," Henry said.

William framed the fish with his hands as he imagined it on the wall. "Scaring all them little school children."

"Give 'em nightmares," James said.

William and James offered to tow the fish to Columbia.

"We can get Sikes to come down with his crane," William said. "Call him on my cell phone. He'll put it on a flatbed truck and haul it to Baxter's cold storage place."

"Big enough for this fish?" Robert asked.

"Plenty of room," James said. "I got me a deer and a wild boar hung up in there right now."

They transferred enough gas from the bass boat to take them to Columbia. Then they tied a line to the fish. The smell of it had changed. Now the stink was that of decay. Robert hoped to have it in cold storage before the sun came up. The bass boat had a hundred horsepower motor. They would be able to quickly cover the remaining distance to the town. James was on the phone to his uncle Sikes, who agreed to meet them with his truck and crane.

Once they had the fish under tow, it was not long before they saw the glow of the town's lights against the night sky. They passed under a highway bridge. The town appeared on a bluff to their left.

James brought the boat into shore where a concrete boat ramp had been built to provide access to the river. His uncle Sikes was waiting with the crane and a flatbed truck.

"I called Baxter," Sikes said. "He's opening up for us." Sikes then turned to the man standing beside him. "Come on, Davy, let's go look at that fish. Maybe these boys have been out on the river drinking whiskey. Maybe they ain't got nothing at all."

"They probably got somebody's dead hog," Sikes said.

"I don't smell no hog," Davy said.

"You come look," William said. "I'll show you what these boys have got." He turned the spotlight on the bass boat onto the fish.

"Lord!" Sikes said. "Look at that!"

"Let's get to work," Davy said. "I don't want to be around that thing when the sun comes up and it starts to stink." Davy spotted Hoffman. "They got their own buzzard too. Waiting for it to get rotten enough to suit him."

They wound cables around the fish and then Sikes used the crane to lift it onto the flatbed truck. The fish lay on its side with its mouth open. Paul stood beside it, gazing into one of its eyes.

"Eat a man in one bite," Sikes said. "I sure hope its mamma don't live some place where I fish."

They climbed into James' and William's pickups and followed the truck though the sleeping town to the cold storage house. Sikes lifted the fish off the truck and placed it on three dollies they had set side by side. When they opened the doors, the cold air spilled out of the room, forming clouds of fog about the door. They rolled the dollies into the room, and left the fish amid sides of beef and deer and wild boar.

"I'm not going back on the river until I drink a cold one," Mason said.

Everyone agreed that a cold beer would be a fine thing. So Sikes drove them to a convenience store that stayed open all night. They filled the gas tanks from the John boats and then drove back through the deserted streets to the boat launching ramp, where they sat in the beds of the pickups and drank cold beer and listened to the radio of William's truck.

Mason had insisted on buying beer in bottles. Robert drank from a bottle, which was sweaty in his hand from the heat. The beer felt good going down. He held the bottle against his cheek, savoring the coldness. He thought of the big fish, slowly turning rigid in the storage room. He drank a second bottle and then a third. Mason walked back to the truck where Robert was sitting, leaving Paul standing by the river.

"Paul's staying here," he said.

"You mean he's going home?" Robert asked.

"I suppose," he said.

Paul walked over to the truck, and they all drank to his departure. William offered to let him sleep at his house.

"Have you got a place I can keep Hoffman?" Paul asked.

"Sure, out where my wife used to have chickens," William said. "Coons and foxes can't get at him there."

"You can take a hot shower," Mason said. "Think of that."

"And sleep in air conditioning," Henry said. "You got that William?"

"Sure do," William said. "We like to turn it down real low and sleep under blankets."

They all shook hands with Paul. Then they loaded the gas and remaining beer and flour and coffee and grits into the boats. Mason piloted his boat alone.

They ran under the second highway bridge below the town just as the sun was rising. Mason studied the maps and told them that there were no towns between this place and Bougalosa. Only at a few points did a dirt road lead down to the river.

"It's gonna get wilder the closer we get to the Gulf," Mason said. "A paradise of snakes and gators."

They ran for an hour and made camp on a sandbar. It was already hot. Everyone went to sleep. As Robert lay under the tarp, he thought of Octavius and Mary, each covered with mud, sleeping in the pirogue; he thought of Paul, sleeping beneath a blanket at William's house; he thought of the gar, which had once pro-

pelled its streamlined body through the warm water, slowly turning rigid. He imagined the whole river, past, present, and future
congealing in some vast ice house, they and the fish and Octavius
locked together. Only in death could anything be preserved:
Octavius' words on paper and the gar hanging on a museum wall,
dry and lifeless, its soft bones brittle to the touch. When he woke
he planned on returning to the manuscript. They would hunt and
eat, returning to that familiar rhythm, and that night, surrounded
by the drone of the insects and the calls of the night birds, he
would read to them of Octavius.

Chapter Sixteen

THEY RAN UNDER power all afternoon while Robert worked on
the manuscript. He was relieved Paul was gone. He imagined Elizabeth driving down to Columbia, a trip of not much over an hour.
Paul would have showered and shaved and had a good night's sleep
at William's house. Paul and Elizabeth would go home and make
love. He would be all right.

Mason's boat sheared a pin on a snag, and they stopped to
repair it.

"I wonder how Elizabeth is gonna take to that buzzard?" Mason said.

"Not at all," said Henry.

"I think Hoffman'll end up at the Jackson zoo," Robert said.

Mason finished replacing the pin. They got underway again.

Robert concentrated on the manuscript. Mason ran his boat
with a rifle across his knees. But so far he had spotted no game.

The deer were up in the trees, lying still during this hottest
part of the day. They had run by a couple of big gators, but Mason
passed up the shots. It was not necessary for them to eat gator
meat. No one was particularly fond of it, even when it was smothered in barbecue sauce. So far they had not gone hungry, and he
did not expect this day to be any different.

Late in the afternoon they came upon a raccoon digging a hole
on a sandbar. The raccoon ran for the trees and disappeared.

"Turtle eggs," Mason said.

They went ashore and discovered a series of nests. They filled two buckets with the eggs.

"Nothing's better than turtle eggs," Mason said. "My daddy taught me how to dig eggs."

Robert imagined the father and the boy digging the eggs out of the warm sand and how Mason might have hefted the first egg he found in his hand, the leathery shell smooth against his palm.

"Pap and me fried them eggs in an iron skillet," Mason recalled. He remembered watching his father take the eggs out of the sand and hiss of the lard in the iron skillet. It was one of the few times he could ever recall being proud of something his father had done. "That was before he got sick."

Mason said that his father had died of TB. Robert knew that sometimes people died of that in America but not many. It had become a disease of impoverished populations. It was a disease that seemed to Robert to belong in the nineteenth century.

"Pap would take them pills for awhile." Mason knelt before one of the holes they had dug in the sand. He ran his fingers through the loose sand, searching for any eggs they might have missed. "Then he'd start drinking again. He was bad to take a drink."

No one said anything. Henry thought of his father who drove a garbage truck in Jackson. He had started as one of those workers who picked up cans. Now his father was retired. They had fished and hunted together and he could recall dozens of experiences like the one Mason had just described. Robert knelt beside Mason. Mason stopped his search.

"We'll have turtle eggs for supper," Robert said. "You show us how to cook them."

They came upon another irrigation pump and decided to raid the farmer's field. Mason and Henry went. Henry carried a shotgun. He was hoping to walk up a covey of quail or shoot a few doves. Robert continued to work on the translation.

For a time the noise of the pump bothered him but then he was able to ignore it and worked steadily.

They returned with corn and guinea hens. Mason held three by their feet. Henry carried a sack of corn.

"We're gonna eat good tonight," Mason said. "Henry sure is a good shot."

"Let's go," Henry said. "Those birds belong to somebody."

They ran down the river. Robert cleaned the fowl as they traveled, the handfuls of feathers he plucked swept away by the wind.

Late in the afternoon they made camp. Mason took charge of the dinner. He cut the birds into pieces, shook them in a bag filled with flour, and fried them in an iron skillet over the butane stove. They shucked the corn and tossed the ears into a pot set to boil over the fire. Once the birds had been fried and were set to drip on paper towels, Mason made an omelet out of the turtle eggs.

They drank whiskey and sat around the fire, listening to the calls of the night birds. When a gator grunted from off in the swamp, Mason grunted back. The gator did not return the call.

"You need more practice," Henry said.

"If I stayed on the river the rest of my life," Mason said, "I'd get all the practice I'd need."

"There's no cold beer on this river," said Henry.

"I could do without that," Mason said.

"You sure?" Robert asked.

"Maybe I could spent a few nights in the towns. What I mean is that I wish this river were a million miles long and there were no towns. Just us and the woods and the animals."

"What about winter?" Henry asked.

"It'd be a river without winter," Mason said.

"A Garden of Eden?" Robert asked.

"Not that," Mason said. "I don't want that. Too many serpents in them gardens. Besides I want animals to hunt and fish to catch."

"Read to us, Robert," Henry said.

"I'm going to miss Paul speaking it to us," Robert said.

Everyone was silent for a moment as they thought about Paul. They all hoped he was with Elizabeth now.

Robert picked up the manuscript and began to read.

Swimming the River

I talked to Mary of how it would be when we reached Haiti. I spoke of the white house on the green hill above the blue sea, of a garden full of flowers, a perpetual riot of color. And I spoke of love. I told her that we might find it necessary to kill other people to reach that green hill, but that once we were there love would heal us. Our children would be free of any contagion.

I thought I felt for her something like what I had felt for Strode Maury. But was that love? I was not sure. Was it truly love, the sort of love of which the poets sang?

But Mary did not speak to me of love. She spoke only of the child whom I had entombed in the cypress. It appeared to be the single idea of which she was capable of thinking, and I began to fear that she was descending into madness. I was concerned that she might betray us at some point by an impulsive act.

She began to demand we examine every hollow cypress we came upon. The first few times I willingly submitted and even crawled into the bowels of one with her and watched her run her fingers over the surface of the wood, searching for the spot where I had walled up the child with clay. Once we went deep into a swamp and made our way out of that labyrinth back to the river again only because I had taken a compass bearing.

I thought that once we reached Haiti she would be well. There would be other children; the memory of the child would fade as she turned her love to them. Each morning would not bring potential terror but the promise of a day with her children. She would stand with them before the house and watch our cane fields ripple in the steady wind from the sea.

Some nights I would wake from a bad dream or be roused by a strange sound. If it were close to dawn, I would stay awake and watch her sleep. She had begun to sleep very soundly so that sometimes I imagined she was dead. I would put my hand to her lips to feel her breath or lay my head against her mud-coated breast to listen to the beating of her heart.

Then one morning I returned from defecating in the woods to find her and the pirogue gone. She had left me nothing. All I had was a Bowie knife I wore in a leather sheath on a belt. I yelled for her; I screamed. I stood on the sandbar at the mouth of the creek and cried, my tears cutting tracks in the coating of dried mud on my face.

I found a driftwood log and pushed it out into the river. There settling myself upon it I let the current take me. I hoped she might have some difficulty with the pirogue and that I might overtake her. What was important were the charts and sextant and compass, all inside a wooden box that I had lashed to one of the seats. Even if she turned the boat over these would be safe.

All night I clung to the log. Since most of my body was beneath the water, the insects did not trouble me. But I could feel my skin becoming wrinkled like a piece of dried fruit. I watched the stars wheel above my head and the moon rise and fall. Then the morning star began to rise, and the sky turned pink with the coming dawn.

I planned to investigate every creek, for I expected her to follow the custom we had established. If I were lucky, I would catch her asleep in the pirogue.

Then I smelled smoke. I saw it rising from the outside of a bend where I assumed there was a sandbar. I maneuvered the log to that side of the river. It was still dark on the river. I could approach very closely by simply remaining still and letting the current carry me and the log. I had placed my head behind the thickest portion. Anyone looking upriver would see only the outline of a log.

I saw the pirogue and a skiff at the water's edge. A man lay by the fire, but I saw no sign of Mary. I left the log and swam up into the willows. I crawled onto the sand and worked my way closer. Perhaps if the man were sleeping I could kill him with my knife. I had resolved, if I regained my arms, to never be without a pistol or a rifle, no matter what I was doing.

The man lying by the fire was dead. A knot of flies buzzed about him. Someone had shot him just below the right eye. His blood had stained the sand dark. I got up on my knees and saw the others. Near the trees a man lay atop Mary. The flies were about them too. I supposed he had taken her there to be out of the firelight.

I rose and walked over to the dead man. I picked up his rifle and checked to see if it had been fired. It had not. Then, the rifle in my hands, I examined Mary and the other dead man. I supposed they had fought over her, not for love, but for the money she represented, and the man who lay atop her with a Bowie knife in his back had taken her there to enjoy her in the darkness. He had strangled her before he died. His hands had fallen away, but there were bruises on her throat. She must have thought that with one knife thrust she could regain the pirogue again and continue to search for her child.

I did not weep over her. I suppose that it was because I believed she was better off dead. Again I wondered if what I felt for her had been love. But perhaps that was something I had yet to experience. Yet I had imagined the sort of life we might have lived together; she had become part of my dream. I realized that the education I had received had been worthless. As far as I could tell, Mary and I were no more than masked figures in some sort of savage play. We loved and wept and died, but actually we were something else that we ourselves had only an imperfect knowledge of. I was sorry she had to die in such a violent fashion. I was sorry for everyone who had died and it seemed to me that the river and Mississippi was one great charnel house. I buried them all. It was considerable trouble to do so, but I dug deep holes in the sand and one by one slipped them into them.

I found it difficult to push the sand onto her naked body, but I had nothing to cover her with. I did not want to use the men's clothes. So I cut willow branches and dropped them over her until there was a thick green carpet of leaves at the bottom of the grave. I pushed the sand into it.

After I went through their gear and reloaded an empty rifle that must have belonged to the man Mary killed. I built up the fire and made coffee. I had not had a cup of coffee since the day I killed Strode Maury. I sat there in the daylight with the loaded rifles and pistols beside me and drank a whole pot of coffee.

I left the pirogue and took the skiff, which had oars, and went down the river in the daylight with a brace of pistols in my belt and three rifles at my feet. I saw no one that day. When the sun set, I continued until daylight, rowing much of the time to aid the current. I ran the skiff up into a creek and lay down, plastered with mud, to sleep. I hoped I would not dream of Mary, and I did not. Instead I dreamed of the house above the sea. I stood on the porch surrounded by my children. The sea below was covered with white sails.

"It's DIFFERENT WHEN you read it," Henry said.

"You'd rather have Paul back?" asked Robert.

"No," Henry said. "It's just different, but in what way I'm not sure."

They all sat and looked into the fire. No one spoke.

Robert considered telling them the story of *The White Book*. He would start with that and then tell them about Elaine. His love, the two years of grief he had endured. But he wondered what would be the point in that. What was his grief to what Octavius had already experienced. But perhaps it was foolish to try to measure grief. One night as they sat around the fire he would tell them but not now, not immediately after he had read a section of the manuscript.

Henry continued, "How could he survive that? I think he was afraid of loving her. Then she was dead and it was too late."

"Why did he come back to Mississippi?" Robert said. "I would want to forget."

"I would've stayed in Haiti," Mason said. "He was a duke there. I'll bet he had him one of them big white houses he keeps dreaming about."

They sat around the fire and talked of Octavius for a long time. The death of Mary had unnerved Robert. He felt reluctant to take up the rest of the manuscript in the morning. There was enough left for perhaps a week or maybe two of work. Mason and Henry went off to sleep.

Robert thought that he might leave the manuscript alone for a while. Octavius was dreaming of children in the midst of horror. Robert was weary of writing about terror and annihilation. Octavius had gotten himself out of Mississippi, but he was never free. There was no hope for him. He had gone down into that darkness, and no white house in the sunshine on a green hill above the blue sea could save him.

Perhaps that was why Octavius had come back to Mississippi, to deal with those ghosts, to try to make sense out of what had happened to him. Robert wanted to write that down, to tell that story. He wondered if the Duke in *The White Book* was satisfied, if he had bad dreams. Again Robert imagined himself pursuing the poachers through the forest. He was certain that a man like Octavius would have found them and killed them. He thought of Elaine picking up her blue back pack, preparing to go teach a class. It was spring and when she opened the door to go out of the house her body was suddenly suffused with light, her red hair seeming to be on fire. But then he pushed that image out of his mind. Madness lay in remembrances like that.

He threw more wood on the fire. Tonight the mosquitoes were not so bad. The smoke seemed sufficient to keep them away. He lay down and closed his eyes. He wanted to sleep and not dream of Octavius.

Chapter Seventeen

DESPITE HIS RESOLUTION to leave the manuscript alone for a time, he began to work on it at first light, before the others were awake. Then the others got up and they made breakfast.

"I wish Paul were here," Henry said.

"I don't miss that buzzard," Mason said. "Don't see how Paul could stand to sleep with that bird in his tent every night."

But then they all agreed it was better he was off the river. Something had happened to him, but no one was exactly sure exactly what that was.

"He started to look at things too hard," Mason said.

And it seemed to Robert that Mason was right. A person could look at things too hard. He would have to be careful with his interest in Octavius.

Then they were out on the river again. The sky was cloudless. It was going to be a very hot day. As they swung around a bend, Robert turned his attention from the manuscript and noticed that the river had deepened. How much it had deepened would be impossible to know without a sounding line. He imagined the water as fabulously deep, going down fifty, sixty or even a hundred feet.

Robert returned to the manuscript, lost his concentration, and then bent his head over it again. The next time he looked up he saw the figure of a man, shimmering in the heat, on the sandbar. Some object was on the sand beside the man.

166

"What's that?" Henry asked.

Mason picked up the field glasses. "It's Paul. Paul and the skull of that fish." Mason passed the glasses to Robert.

Paul was sitting with his arms around his knees. The skull of the gar, which had been stripped of all its flesh and glistened in the sunlight, rested on the sand beside him. Hoffman was perched on the skull. He spread his injured wing and flapped it slowly.

After they picked Paul up, he explained how he and William had sat in the truck and drunk beer until the sun rose. Then Paul had persuaded William to return to the cold storage house. Paul had cut off the gar's head with a chain saw.

"It was frozen just a little on the outside," Paul said.

They had taken the head to William's house and boiled the flesh off it in a big steel pot set over a butane fire. William used the pot to cook crayfish. He and William sat beside the pot in lawn chairs and drank a mixture of orange juice and moonshine William's cousin had made. They turned the head, which was too large to fit completely in the pot, with an iron pole.

"That flesh just sloughed off," Paul said. "Pretty soon there was nothing but bone and teeth. We propped the mouth open with a coke bottle. That head would float around in that boiling water, that mouth with all those teeth pointing up to the sky. William kept telling me that fish was trying to swallow the sun. Then he'd laugh and laugh."

William's wife had brought them breakfast: grits, eggs, ham, and biscuits. They had honey from William's bees.

"Best meal I've had in a long time. He went down the hives for the honey. Those bees crawled all over William but never stung him a single time. He has a gentle touch with bees."

"You get stung?" Henry asked.

"I tended the head and watched," Paul said. "I'd have been stung for sure."

William had told his wife that he was going to call in sick to help Paul with the head. She got mad and told William that if that was the case then he could fix his own lunch and dinner too. She left to take the children to vacation Bible school. Paul and William had returned to drinking moonshine and orange juice and contemplating the head.

"That's what we did," Paul said. "Contemplated it."

"What'd you discover?" Henry asked.

"I'm not sure," Paul said. "We looked at the teeth. This kind of fish is mostly about teeth."

They all regarded the skull. The teeth glistened in the sunlight.

"We dumped bleach in the water." Paul ran his finger over the skull. "It's beautiful."

Paul explained how William had driven him to a point they believed was farther than the boats could have possibly run. Paul had been waiting for their appearance since midnight.

"You can drive right up to the river," Paul said. "There's a dirt track just beyond the trees."

"Anybody growing watermelons?" Mason asked.

"Maybe, there's a couple of fields back a mile or so," Paul said. "I couldn't tell what was planted in 'em. Might be nothing but soybeans or cotton."

Mason went to raid the fields. Paul went to sleep under the tarp. Henry examined the skull and measured it, writing down his findings in a notebook. Robert started to work on the translation but found he could not concentrate. He began to think about writing down the story of Elaine's death and his grief. That was what Octavius had done, but Robert was not certain what the writing of it had done for Octavius. Robert did think that writing it down would be easier than telling it. One of his companions could read it as they sat around the fire. But he did not think he would write it until after he returned to the house.

Henry was counting the teeth in the lower jaw.

"Do you think that fish could swallow a person?" Robert asked.

"I doubt it," Henry said. "But it sure looks big enough to do it. I guess it could eat a person just the same as an alligator could."

"I'm more afraid of it than an alligator."

"Why?"

"Because you can't see it. It's under water all the time. Waiting down there on the bottom of the river."

Henry had finished counting the teeth and was making a sketch of the head.

"What's Octavius doing?" Henry asked.

"You'll find out tonight."

"Paul will want to start memorizing again. That's going to be bad for him."

"Yes, I think it will."

"But you won't stop him."

"No."

"Because what will you say to him."

"That's right, I have nothing to say. This trip. How we live every day is not that much different from what he's doing. People might think we're all a little crazy."

"I think he'll leave at Bougalosa. That's not much left for him. You're almost done. That'll make an end of it. He'll go home to Elizabeth. He can take that damn fish head and go home."

Robert imagined Paul riding home with Elizabeth in an air-conditioned car, the fish skull reposing in the back seat. One day they would all go to Jackson, and there it would be in the state museum.

Henry went to sleep and Robert tried to sleep too, but he could not get the translation out of his mind. He picked up the manuscript and began to work on a sentence.

Robert worked steadily. Henry turned occasionally and opened his eyes only to drop back into sleep again. Paul slept soundly, the sleep of a small child.

When Robert heard Mason calling out to them, he put down the manuscript and stood up. Henry woke suddenly and glanced about quickly. Mason burst through the tree line. He wore a military helmet. A sword was strapped to his waist. The canvass sacks he carried were full.

He put the sacks down and drew the sword. He pointed his

sword towards Robert and Henry. He charged. "Die Americans!" Mason shouted. "Die!" It was as if he were infantryman making a suicidal assault on an enemy position.

Paul woke suddenly. "What! What! What!"

Henry knelt and put his arm around Paul's shoulders. "It's Mason. Just Mason."

Mason collapsed laughing on the sand, breathing hard. "I've got eggplants. And okra. Tomatoes. Lots of tomatoes. Greens, carrots, and brussel sprouts." Mason continued with a list of almost every vegetable Robert had ever heard of, some whose names he had not expected Mason to know.

"I ain't got all of that," Mason confessed. "But I do have eggplants. We'll have fried eggplant tonight."

"Where'd you get all the Japanese stuff?" Paul asked.

"Out of a cabin," Mason said.

He took a Japanese flag from one of the sacks.

Mason explained that it was a hunting cabin someone had filled with souvenirs from the war in the Pacific.

"He was navy man," Mason said. "There's pictures of his ship all over the cabin."

"You should take it all back," Henry said.

"What does it matter," Mason said "He's an old man now. With one foot in the grave. I've always wanted a samurai sword."

"You should return it," Henry insisted.

"I got whiskey out of that cabin," said Mason. "That man drinks good stuff."

"Mason, you don't understand anything about anything," said Henry.

"You've been breaking the same game laws as the rest of us. You been eating deer and stolen corn. You'll eat stolen eggplant tonight. I don't see the difference."

"I'll take it back," Henry said.

"Nobody's taking anything back," Robert said. "We're going down the river."

"Don't get too attached to that sword," Henry cautioned. "When we get home I'm coming back here. I'll return it to the owner."

"Why not take it to Japan, return it to the real owner's family," Mason said. "Why he might even be alive. He'd be an old man. Make his whole damn day to get his favorite sword back. He'd give you some of that wine they make out of rice. Whiskey. That's what you need. Have a drink and calm down." Mason handed Henry a bottle.

Henry took a drink and praised the quality of the whiskey.

They loaded the boats. Mason lashed the cane pole to which the flag was attached to the canopy frame of his boat.

Robert took a seat beneath the canopy with the manuscript. Paul lay down in the shade. Hoffman sat on his perch and periodically spread and unspread both of his wings at the same time.

"I believe that buzzard may fly again after all," Mason said.

"He will," Henry said. "Paul healed him."

"Paul, is that buzzard gonna fly?" Mason asked.

But Paul did not answer. He was already asleep.

They moved off down the river. For a time Robert sat and watched the river unreel before his eyes, the familiar scenery of water and trees. Then he put his head down and immersed himself in the words of Octavius.

Chapter Eighteen

THEY HAD BASS for dinner. Henry breaded the eggplant and fried it. Everyone but Paul ate. He sat by himself at the downstream end of the sandbar with the translation in his hands. When they called out to him to come eat, he said he did not have time to eat or even to feed Hoffman. Henry offered to feed him, but to everyone's surprise Mason insisted on doing it.

Mason had surprised himself by his offer. Henry and Robert had laughed when he made it, saying that Hoffman surely remembered who had shot him.

"Tell him you want to kiss and make up," Henry said.

"Next thing you know Mason will be wanting Hoffman to sleep in his tent," said Robert.

Mason cut up one of the bass for Hoffman. He held out a piece to the bird who took it gingerly out of his fingers just like he did when Paul fed him. Mason did wonder if Hoffman remembered the shooting. Had Hoffman seen him just as clearly as he had seen the bird through the telescopic sight. At that moment their eyesight was equal. He finished feeding him the fish. Hoffman stretched out both his wings. He was still tethered to his perch by the cord.

"You're gonna fly ain't you," Mason said.

"Listen to that," Robert said. "He sounds just like Paul."

But the bird, now that all the fish was gone, ignored Mason

and fixed his eyes on Paul.

Paul stood at the downstream end of the sandbar with Robert's translation in his hands. He had suddenly discovered that memorizing it had become easy. He felt a great sense of calm. He looked about him, and it was as if he were seeing the river for the first time, as if he were some newly created being who had been deposited on the sandbar by a god. He murmured the names of things: sky, water, sand, tree, cloud. Clarity was ridiculously easy. All he had to do was recite the names.

Then he began to walk back and forth as he practiced his delivery of the latest chapter, every now and then a few words and pieces of sentences drifting up to the group beneath the tarp.

"I can't get over how he can do that so quick," Henry said. "I wonder if there's some connection between being able to do that and lack of sleep."

"He slept in the boat," said Robert.

"Not for long," Mason said. "I don't think he actually sleeps. It's like he's half awake all the time."

At dusk Paul wandered back up to the tarp. Bats twisted in the air. They heard the sound of a train whistle.

"Going down to New Orleans," Mason said.

Henry started a driftwood fire.

Paul gave the manuscript to Robert saying as he did, "I can do it backwards."

"I don't believe that," Mason said.

Henry took the manuscript and graded Paul as he attempted a paragraph. Paul stumbled about some but completed it.

"Close, very close," Henry said. "When did you know you could do that?"

"Last night when I was sitting on the sandbar with the skull. I spoke the first chapter. I spoke the whole thing backwards and forward. I walked up and down to keep the mosquitoes off me and spoke it."

"Don't you spook Mason and start saying the Lord's Prayer backwards," Henry said.

"Let him go ahead and do it," Mason said. "I know he ain't the devil. He ain't even talked with the devil. Just that bird."

Robert started to say something to calm Paul but then he began to recite the new section.

The Sea

One night I floated out of the forest and into a place where there was marsh on both sides of the river. I smelled the sea in the air. In the morning I ran the boat up into a creek and hid in the tall green grass. The creek was full when I entered it, but then the water dropped as the tide turned.

I had a piece of deer meat that had gone rancid. I tied it to a string and used it to catch crabs, which were abundant in the creek. I ate them raw, cracking the claws and shells open with my knife and sucking the meat out of them.

Now as I traveled I saw the occasional lights of watermen, out fishing on the river. I lay flat in the skiff and hoped they would not see me. Fortunately the moon was just a sliver of light in the night sky. I did not believe they would see me by starlight. They were blinded by their own lights. I feared coming upon someone with no lights. I planned to lie in the bottom of the skiff with pistols in my hands and hope that if I were discovered I could kill them all.

The river grew wider and wider until I was sure that the sea was very close. I spent the day hiding in the marsh. Not far away I saw two men using a cast net. They were both black men, and I wondered if they were slaves or free. The one who threw the net sang a song as he pulled it in, but I could not make out the words. That night I rowed down river as the rising tide swelled to fill the creeks and marsh. I was desperate to find a boat to steal under the cover of darkness. And now I feared that I might be swept out to sea. In the morning I would find myself exposed with no place to hide if I could not overcome the currents with the oars.

During the period when the tide was full but before it had begun to turn, I came upon a two-masted sloop moored at the mouth of a big creek. The sloop was dark, and I supposed the owners were asleep or gone ashore. I made for the water next to the bank, pulling hard on the oars. Then I used an oar to pole the skiff up into the mouth of the creek.

For a time I sat in the skiff and listened for any sounds coming from the sloop. At first there was nothing, but then I heard a man's voice and then a woman's. Sounds of love, sighs and murmurs, began to come from the sloop. I sculled the skiff across the creek and made the bow fast to their anchor chain. To my surprise I found another skiff tied there.

I sat and listened again to their sighs. It was going to be a hard thing to kill them, but there was no other way. The man would capture me if I gave him a chance, and I would be executed in some terrible way for my crimes.

I went up the anchor chain, the pistols in belt, and worked my way across the deck and then down the stairs into the cabin. I pushed opened the jalousied door. It was as if I was lying in the bed with them. They no longer were talking. I heard the sound of his body against hers and their breathing.

I slid across that polished teak floor like a snake. Now I smelled the scent of sex. The cabin was full of it. I followed the sounds of love to them.

I lay next to the bunk until I had located their heads and feet. I rose up, cocked both pistols and pushed them against their heads and pulled the triggers. The pistols went off with a flash, which allowed me to see the two of them frozen for an instant in the light, a dark-haired man atop a blonde-haired women. The report and smoke filled the cabin. I pulled the Bowie in case it was necessary to complete my work.

It was not. They were both still. I found a candle on the table and a match to light it. The cabin filled with light, and I looked at them lying together on the bunk. They were both young, as young as I was. I drew a sheet over them.

I examined the boat and found provisions for a journey. There were water casks and hardtack along with fresh vegetables. When I returned to the cabin, I found a sextant and a compass and charts of the Gulf. I opened a small chest and found woman's clothing and a packet of letters.

As I sat at the table and read them, I discovered they were from the man, Richard Desmond He had written them to the woman, Sally Hall. Desmond lived in New Orleans. He was a Creole who had fallen in love with Sally, but her father had forbidden the marriage. The letters from Desmond were passionate and full of declarations of his love and descriptions of what their life in New Orleans would be like. He came from a wealthy family, and he spoke of the house *where they would live after the marriage and of the beautiful gardens filled with flowers.*

I read his letter to her setting up the assignation that had brought them to the mouth of this creek. Her father had a house on this creek, and she had rowed down it to meet him. He had come up the river on the rising tide and met her. There as they had waited for the ebbing tide to carry them down the river and out into the Gulf they had started to make love. In a few days they would have been in New Orleans, well beyond the reach of her father.

I transferred everything from my skiff to the sloop. Then I knocked holes in the bottoms of both skiffs and sank them. Already the tide was turning, and the sloop was being tugged toward the Gulf, restrained only by the anchor.

I planned to bury them at sea. If there was pursuit on the part of Sally's father, then it would be in the direction of New Orleans.

When I went up on deck to bring up the anchor, I found myself thinking of Mary. If she were here, we would be going down the river together. Mary and I could have taken their places in that bunk. But I knew that I must push Mary out of my mind. In Haiti there would be other women, and I would build that white house on a hill above the sea. I held onto that idea like a sailor whose boat had been sunk might cling to a shattered spar as he was tossed by monstrous seas.

The ebbing tide took the sloop, and I went down the river in the darkness. I saw the lights of a few fisherman. Once a man hailed the sloop from a skiff, but I said nothing in reply, and soon I left his cries far behind me.

*At sunrise I reached the mouth of the river,
the Gulf opening up before me wide and blue between twin headlands, seeming to stretch on forever. The water as far as I could see in either
direction was clear of sails.*

*I brought the bodies up from the cabin and
wrapped each in a fine cotton sheet. I was sorry
that I had nothing to weight them with. I had no
prayer book to use to say words over them. I said
a prayer for their souls, thinking as I spoke the
words, that my soul was beyond the reach of
prayers. If I perished at sea during my journey,
there would be no one to pray for me.*

*I took out the charts and set a compass
course that would take me out past the barrier
islands and toward Haiti. I hoisted the sails,
which bellied out in the freshening breeze, and
took the helm of the sloop. For the first time in
my life I was free. I felt the power of the wind
through the wheel. Porpoise appeared off the
starboard bow. They frolicked in the bow wave
as I sailed into the morning light.*

"HE'S FREE," Henry said. "He had to kill all those people, but
he's free."

Henry imagined Octavius lying down to sleep in the same bunk
where Sally and Richard had lain. He would have lashed the wheel
in place and shortened his sail. Henry wondered what Octavius
might have dreamed on those tropical nights, alone beneath the
stars, sailing that dark water streaked with phosphorescence.

"If Mary had lived, he wouldn't have returned," said Paul.

"How come?" Mason asked.

"I don't know," Paul said. "It's just a feeling I have. They'd
have raised a family. She'd have known what his life had been
like. She'd have understood him."

"He came back," Robert said. "He bought the house his former master and lover had built, the man he killed with a Bowie knife. Then he sat down and wrote that story. Everyone in the county knew that Octavius had done it. Why didn't someone kill him?"

"Strode Maury had no friends," Henry said. "He left no heirs. His affair with that boy was a perversion. Everyone saw his death as sort of divine justice. That's what I've always thought."

"They'd have killed him later," Robert said. "Or driven him away. His crime then would've been simply that he was a black man."

"I think he imagined a different sort of Mississippi," Henry observed. "He was mistaken."

They sat about the fire and talked of Octavius until it was past midnight. Then one by one they drifted off to their tents. Paul was left sitting by the fire with Hoffman.

"You're going to fly off and never return," Paul said.

Hoffman looked intently at him.

"And I'll think that every turkey vulture I see is you."

Hoffman stretched out his wings.

"But it's not quite time yet. You need to be perfect again. Then you'll soar."

The bird put his head under his wing and went to sleep.

Paul did not feel sleepy at all. He began to say the last chapter backwards. As Robert drifted off to sleep, he imagined Elizabeth driving Paul home while he recited the manuscript to her and the gar skull reposed in the back seat.

Chapter Nineteen

ROBERT PULLED ON his shorts and stepped out of the tent. He smelled coffee. Paul was sitting by the fire. The waterproof bag, which held the manuscript, was on the sand beside him. Hoffman sat on the perch. The bird stretched his wings wide and exercised them. Although Paul had taken off the splint, Hoffman still wore his tether. There was a piece of red bandana tied around one of his legs.

"Hoffman is almost ready to fly," Paul said. "The bone probably wasn't even cracked."

"What's the bandana for?" Robert asked.

"So I can tell him from any other vulture after he flies off. I think he'll stay with me. I don't ever expect him to leave."

Robert picked up the waterproof bag. It was empty. "Where's my manuscript?"

"I burned it," Paul said calmly.

"Damn you, you had no right!"

"You don't need it. You've got me." Paul tapped the side of his head with his forefinger.

Robert hit Paul in the face with a straight left hand. Paul swung at him and missed. Then Robert was on top of him. They rolled about on the tarp, their arms about each other, neither one of them able to gain an advantage.

Then Robert felt other hands on him. Henry held him while

180

Mason wrapped his arms about Paul.

"I can speak it all," Paul said. "Anytime I want. I'll record it for you when we get home. You've got nothing to worry about. I'm not trying to take if from you. I love you, Robert. I love all of you."

Paul embraced him and Robert hugged him back. Paul was crying.

"It's here in my head," Paul said. "Anytime you want it."

They ate a breakfast of grits and sliced tomatoes. Paul had a bruise on his cheek. Robert had a sore rib. He felt embarrassed by his reaction to the destruction of the manuscript.

Paul offered to repeat any chapter Robert chose to prove that his memory was perfect. Robert told him that he believed him, that he had perfect confidence in his ability.

"I'll say it and you'll write it down," Paul said. "And this time you'll understand Octavius like I understand him."

They loaded the boats and were out on the river again. It felt strange to Robert not to have the manuscript before him.

"You can translate it again if Paul forgets," Henry said. "It'll be easy the second time."

At noon they stopped on a sandbar. They were close to Bougalosa and had begun to smell the stink of the paper mill. Paul walked to the down stream end and returned to announce that a tower was built in the middle of the river. Mason looked on his maps but there was no indication of it.

Henry and Mason and Robert took a boat to look at it. No one, not even Henry, had much of an idea of its original function. A rusted metal ladder ran up one side of it, passing over several square openings. Henry speculated that it might have been a pier for a bridge or that it was built as a pylon to carry lines across the river when electricity first came to this part of Mississippi.

Henry went up the ladder to take a look.

"Be careful," Mason said. "Some of those rungs may have rusted through."

Henry went up to the first opening and peered inside. Then he came down the ladder fast.

"What is it?" Robert asked.

"I don't know what it was once," Henry said. "But right now it's a giant hornet nest. There must be a million of 'em in there."

They pulled carefully away from the tower and returned to the sandbar. Robert put out lines for catfish off the sandbar but had no luck. Paul came and fished too. He wanted fresh meat for Hoffman.

"Too bad," Mason said, who walked out of the shade of the tarp to observe the fishing. "Looks like that buzzard will eat deer jerky like the rest of us."

Paul gave up on fishing and went back to the tarp where he talked with Henry. One by one they abandoned fishing and returned to the shade of the tarp. There they ate the jerky and drank warm water. When Paul offered Hoffman a piece, the vulture was not interested.

"Not ripe enough for him," Mason said.

"He wants it fresh," said Paul.

"Don't we all," Mason said.

Mason walked out from beneath the tarp and looked up at the cloudless blue sky. "This day is about as hot as any we've had. I think we should stay right here. We can run at night."

"Too dangerous," Robert said.

"Too many snags," said Henry.

"Yawl are about the most careful people I've ever seen," Mason observed.

Mason took up the Mannlicher and a box of ammunition.

"I reckon I can borrow this if I bring back some meat," Mason said.

"Go ahead," Robert said. "Hunting won't be easy. Deer'll be bedded down in the thickets."

"Well, you never know," Mason said.

Mason walked off toward the down river end of the sandbar with the rifle. They all went to sleep under the tarp.

Robert slept and dreamed of Octavius, who was sailing the boat across the blue Gulf towards Haiti. Robert saw the green island rising out of the sea, the air over it filled with enormous, brilliantly colored birds.

The crack of the Mannlicher brought Robert out of his dream. It woke the others too. The firing, which came from the end of the sandbar, continued.

"What's that fool doing?" Henry asked.

"Shooting up all my ammunition," Robert said.

Still Mason continued to fire, the sound of the shots echoing against the trees. Robert and Henry went to investigate.

They found Mason at the end of the sandbar shooting at the tower. He shot one last time before Robert snatched the rifle away from him.

"How are we going to pass that tower now?" Robert asked.

Mason grinned. "We're not."

"Those hornets might not be calmed down by morning," said Henry.

"We can slip right by 'em after dark," Mason said. "They can't fly in the dark."

They left Mason sitting on the sand and returned to the tarp.

"Maybe he's right," Robert said. "It would be cooler at night."

"Down below Bougalosa, we can run at night," Henry said. "There're just too many snags on this part of the river."

"We'd have to go so slowly it wouldn't be worth doing," Robert said. "We'll wait until dark and run by. We'll camp again at the first good place we come to."

They all lay down to sleep again.

Henry woke Robert from a dreamless sleep.

"Look," Henry said.

Paul had poled one of the boats out into the river. He was wearing rain gear, which must have been intolerably hot in the afternoon heat. Hoffman sat on his perch. Paul had removed his tether.

Mason woke. He looked about him and ran to the edge of the water, calling out to Paul. Paul ignored his cries and started the motor and went down the river, leaving Mason standing knee deep in the water He continued to yell at Paul as the boat disappeared around the end of the sandbar.

When Mason started up the motor of the remaining boat, Robert and Henry went to join him. By the time they caught up with Paul he was close to the tower. He had put up the hood of his rain jacket. Mason stopped their boat and turned back when a hornet stung him on the cheek. He ran the boat back upriver and put in close to the bank in the shade of a big poplar.

"Look!" Henry said. "He did it. He healed him just like he said he would."

Hoffman had taken flight. He turned in circles over the river, soaring close to the treetops. Paul was watching him.

"I'd gain some altitude," Mason said as he rubbed his cheek. "Put some distance between me and them hornets."

A group of hornets flew past them upriver before turning and circling back to the tower.

Paul had reached the tower. Now he was wearing something over his face. Mason picked up the field glasses and looked at Paul.

"He cut the mosquito netting out of his tent," Mason said. "He's made himself a beekeeper's suit."

Paul tied the bow line to the ladder. Then he began to climb the ladder.

"What's he doing?" Mason asked.

Henry had the glasses. "He's taking a rope up the tower."

Paul had rope tied to his belt. It was paying out as he climbed the ladder. When Paul reached the second opening, he stopped. He pulled on rope, which was attached to a can of gasoline.

"Gonna burn 'em out," Mason said. "That's good."

Paul pulled the can up to his position.

"Give it to those little bastards," Mason said.

Robert watched Paul through the field glasses.

"What's he doing now?" Mason asked. "What's he waiting for?"

Paul had something in his left hand, but Robert could not make it out. The enormous form of Hoffman swooped into his field of vision.

"What's he doing?" Henry asked. "Give me those."

He snatched the field glasses out of his hand.

Robert looked at Paul atop the tower. Hoffman had gained altitude and turning in tight circles.

"You tell me," Robert said to Henry.

"I can't see," Henry said.

"Let me," Mason said, reaching for the field glasses.

Then there was a hard explosion, followed by a second softer one. Paul and the tower disappeared in a ball of flame. Hoffman shot upward on the rising air from the explosion before he disappeared in the smoke. A moment later a hot wind blew over them.

"Paul!" Henry cried.

"My dynamite!" Mason shouted. "He took my dynamite!"

Mason started the motor. They were there in a few seconds. A gasoline stink was in the air, and everywhere the charred remains of hornets littered the water. One side of the tower had been blown off. It had fallen on the boat and the gas in the boat's tanks had ignited, blowing the boat apart. What was left of it drifted upside down in the water, held afloat by the flotation under the seats.

They found Paul floating face down in the river. His mosquito net mask had been torn from his face. The front of the rain suit had been shredded by the explosion and melted by the fire.

Henry began to cry as Robert and Mason pulled the body into the boat. Robert took the canopy off its frame and wrapped the body in it.

"Look, there's that damn Hoffman," Mason said.

Overhead, Hoffman flew in smooth, slow circles.

"You won't get Paul!" Mason shouted.

Mason took up his .22 and began to shoot at Hoffman, putting up rounds as fast as he could pull the trigger, the brass cases falling in a bright stream and rattling on the bottom of the boat. Then the magazine was empty and Hoffman, who had not appeared even to notice he was being shot at, still turned overhead.

"Leave him alone," Robert said. "He's just an animal."

They returned to the sandbar.

"What happened?" Henry asked.

"I'm not sure," Robert said. "He made a mistake."

"Maybe the gasoline went off when he started to light the fuse," Henry said.

"We'll never know," Mason said. "Let the county coroner figure it out as best he can."

"Let's go to Bougalosa," Robert said.

Robert felt that he was responsible. He was the one who had organized the trip. Explaining to Elizabeth what had happened to Paul was going to be the hardest thing he had ever done, even harder than going to Africa to retrieve Elaine's body. And now he felt an impulse to tell them about Elaine, about his friend Peter and *The White Book*. Then together they might try to understand why the forces that ruled the world seemed to be madness and death. He was beginning to wonder if there was any such thing as love, if truly it had been an invention of the troubadours.

They went down past the still smoking tower. A few hornets buzzed about, scouts who had been sent out to investigate the source of the shooting and now had returned to the paper nests which had vanished.

As they went down the river, all exposed to the sun because of the loss of the canopy, Hoffman, flying in huge circles that overlapped their progress, followed them.

Chapter Twenty

No one spoke as they ran under power down the river. Every now and then Robert looked up to see if Hoffman was still there. He was, only the circle he was flying around them was larger. Through the field glasses it was easy to see the bit of red bandana Paul had tied around his leg. In a few weeks it would rot off or Hoffman might pull it off this very day with his beak just before he settled down to sleep with his own kind. They traveled into the sulfuric stink from the paper mill. Robert breathed deeply, letting the smell fill him. Since it was impossible to avoid, he would accustom himself to it. He wondered what Hoffman smelled, if the stink was strong where he flew.

The canvas-shrouded form of Paul lay on the bottom of the boat. Henry sat at his feet, next to Robert. Mason sat at his head. Mason held the .22 as if he hoped to sooner or later get another shot at Hoffman.

Robert wondered what it would be like to bury Paul in the river. That is what Octavius would have done, having passed out of the reach of all order, living by expediency without sheriff or inquest, but at the same time faced with the necessity of judging himself at every turn. If they had buried Paul in the river, Robert imagined himself saying a few words and then they would slip his canvas-wrapped corpse, perhaps weighted with an extra battery, into some deep hole. But the turtles and catfish would pick his bones in the end.

Instead they were taking Paul to Bougalosa, where he would be delivered into the hands of sheriff and coroner. There would be an investigation. Once that was settled Paul would be buried in Jackson. Paul's people were from Jackson. Robert would have to speak to Elizabeth.

First they saw the smoke from the paper mill and then the town. They passed under a highway bridge. Robert put the boat into shore beneath the bridge.

Mason still held the .22 and was looking up at the sky. There was no sign of Hoffman. "I'll stay with Paul."

"That bird's gone," Robert said.

"Maybe. But he could be making one of them big circles. He comes back here and fools with Paul I'll kill him."

Robert wondered if Hoffman had simply flown so high that he was out of sight. He could be up there at this moment, looking down on them with his marvelous eyesight, waiting to reveal himself at his pleasure.

"Don't you be shooting that rifle around the town," Henry said. "One person has already died."

Mason pointed up at the sky. "I'm shooting up there. There's not but one thing that's gonna die."

They walked up to the bridge and bought beer at a gas station. Henry tossed one down to Mason.

"Maybe that'll keep his mind off Hoffman," Henry said.

Robert stood at the approach to the bridge and turned in a circle, searching the cloudless blue sky for Hoffman. It was empty. He called the sheriff at a pay phone. Soon there were three cars next to the boat, along with an ambulance from the local funeral home.

At the sheriff's office they made their statements. There'd be an inquest. They might have to return to Bogalousa for that.

"Who's going to call Elizabeth?" Henry asked.

"I will," Robert said. "I thought up this trip."

He placed the call to Elizabeth and told her Paul had been killed. He did not explain the details, just said it was an accident.

She said that her sister could drive her to Bougalosa. He found it difficult to hang up the phone. It was not enough to say that he was sorry. He kept waiting for her to break down, but she never did. He wanted to tell her about Elaine, to tell her that it might be better if she howled, screamed, and tore her hair. He wanted to advise her to tell everyone of her grief. Henry called his wife. She would drive down.

"I'm going to finish this," Robert said.

"I've had enough," Henry said. "I'd be thinking about Paul the whole time."

"I'll be thinking about Paul too," Robert said. "I want to finish what I've started."

Mason handed Robert the .22. "Shoot that buzzard if you see it."

"I wonder what drove him mad?" Robert said.

Henry thought it was lack of sleep, and they all discussed that for a time. Robert waited for one of them to mention Octavius, but no one brought that up. And Robert thought that he was going to say it, but to his surprise he did not. He supposed that if he had then he might not have been so willing to complete the journey.

"I remember when I killed that buzzard," Mason said. "We didn't see any game all day."

"It was hot," Henry said. "Paul was depriving himself of sleep. And maybe there were things we didn't know about him."

"Yes," Robert said, "Elizabeth might be able to explain what happened."

"Elizabeth," Mason said, "You think she can? Yawl remember him climbing up that tower with them hornets swarming. What's Elizabeth or anyone else going to know about that?"

"Not sleeping makes folks crazy," Henry said.

"He wasn't crazy," Mason said. "It was something else."

"Don't talk to me about somethings," Henry said. "Next thing you know you'll be talking to me about ghosts."

"Yes," Robert said, "he got in the habit of not sleeping. It could have happened to anyone."

"Ha," Mason said. "I don't want to listen to anymore of this. But you watch yourself on that river."

Mason put his arms about Robert and gave him a hug. Henry did the same. They both smelled of sweat and a little of the gar.

Robert filled the gas cans and bought fresh provisions at the store attached to the gas station. He rigged the canopy again. The undertaker's people had left the canvas when they had slipped Paul into a body bag.

By the time he were ready to leave it was late afternoon. He imagined that by this time the others were already on their way home. He looked up at the bridge. He could picture Paul standing on the bridge, worried about Hoffman. Robert looked up at the sky. Right now the bird could be there, so high he could not see him. But Hoffman could see him. Or he could be following the car, riding the thermals high above the road. He could see all the way to Jackson if he flew high enough. They would never be able to drive so far or fast that he could not see. Hoffman could become an unseen spectator at Paul's funeral, looking down from a great height at the spectacle on the grass.

Robert imagined returning to the house. He would translate the manuscript again. They would find a new fourth for doubles. Everything would be the same as they all settled into the pattern of their lives. Henry teaching and counting the years until his retirement; Mason living in the trailer with his mother and grandmother with no prospects and railing against his lot in life. Those days on the river had brought them a different sort of life; they had stepped out of the ordinary into the flow of something else, becoming hunters of the mystery of Octavius. But Paul had paid dearly for the experience. One day after tennis he might tell them about Elaine.

But right now he would focus on going to Haiti. He was not ready to abandon the search for the trail of Octavius just yet.

Robert started the motor. He turned the boat out into the current. A few miles down river the sulfur smell vanished. The wind was carrying it away. He made good time, running between thickly-forested banks. Then it was dusk. He began to look for a good place to camp.

Chapter Twenty-One

ROBERT WOKE IN the morning to a silent camp. Now he wished he had persuaded one of them to go with him. It was still cool from an early morning rain and patches of mist hung low over the river. He fried bacon on the butane stove and made a pot of grits.

He sat under the tarp and ate. From time to time he searched the sky for Hoffman, but the bird did not appear. In Gulfport he planned to buy a boat that would be easy for one man to run, or he might hire someone to make the trip with him. He would have to wait to translate the remaining chapters when he returned home. But he could drive to Jackson and retrieve the manuscript. If he hired someone to run the boat, then it would be easier to work on the new translation during the voyage.

A boat passed by on the river and then another one. He waved to them from the sandbar.

He got out Mason's maps and began to study them.

The river was going to be full of boats from now on. He was not going to be able to live like Octavius with them around. So he decided to leave the river and go to the Gulf through the delta. The Bouge Chitto River came in from the west. It paralleled the Pearl and then with the addition of other bayous became the West Pearl. A maze of bayous and tidal creeks and marshes, bounded on one side by the Pearl and the other by the West Pearl, stretched all the way to the Gulf. He could enter the Gulf through the Old Pearl or the West Pearl.

It would take longer, but it would be worth it. He had not really lived as Octavius did. Paul had come the closest. He would leave all the canned food and tents and as much of the twentieth century as he could on the sandbar. The motor too.

On the map he located a creek, which drained into the river from the labyrinth of marshes and swamps. That was where he would leave everything behind. He studied the map, tracing the path he would take to paddle and pole the boat through the maze of waterways.

As he ran down the river toward the creek, he passed several more boats: bass fishermen, commercial fishermen, whose hoop nets were piled high in their boats, and a group of boy scouts in canoes. He located the creek and ran the boat up into it.

At a sandbar near the mouth he unloaded the boat, stripping it of the motor, gas cans, battery—every modern piece of gear. He kept a compass and the maps, for Octavius had better devices for navigation than he. He kept knives, his guns, the field glasses, a cooking pot and an iron skillet, matches, salt and pepper and a little flour.

He left the gar head. Someone might take it with him when he discovered the valuable things. It would end up on the wall of some crossroads store along with deer heads and rattlesnake skins. Or it might be left and the next high water would bear it away where it would rest undisturbed at the bottom of the river.

The museum in Jackson would end up with the body of the gar. Someone might reproduce the head, perhaps making it even larger than the original. He knew that he would never go to look at it.

He found a vein of clay in a bank and stripping off his clothes covered himself with mud. Then he poled the boat up the creek. The creek began to spread out, and he entered a cypress swamp. He poled the boat through patches of duckweed, the buttressed trees rising tall around him. Every now and then he stopped and took a compass bearing to make sure he was headed in the right direction. Everywhere there were alligators. But he was not interested in gator meat.

Suddenly ahead the water was broken by swimming animals, which he at first thought were beavers. Then he realized they were nutria. He killed one on the first shot with the Mannlicher. The others dived and did not appear again.

He fished the nutria out of the water. It had webbed paws, the huge orange incisors of a beaver, and a long, rat-like tail. He gutted it and threw the entrails into the water. He looked up at the sky. It was too bad that Hoffman was gone. He had missed a good meal.

He came out of the stand of cypress and into an expanse of marsh. Everywhere the tall green grass was cut with channels. He spent the rest of the morning moving through the channels, following a compass bearing to the south. Twice he stopped and replastered himself with mud. A swarm of flies hung over the carcass of the nutria, which he had placed belly side down to keep them off the meat. At noon he stopped at a tiny island in the marsh where live oak and bay and pine had taken root. In the shade of a live oak he built a fire and skinned the nutria. He spitted it over the fire, and he sat, after he had replastered himself with mud, and waited for it to cook.

He wished he had some spices. He imagined rubbing olive oil into the meat and cooking it with thyme and rosemary. Some garlic would be good too.

He looked off toward the stand of cypress, which was now a thin greenish line against the horizon. A group of vultures circled the marsh, so far away they he could barely make out what they were. Perhaps one of them was Hoffman. But the vultures came no closer, instead moving off in the other direction until he lost sight of them, the dark specks they had been reduced to dancing in and out of his field of vision.

The nutria was done. He ate the strong-tasting meat.

In a few days, a week at the most, he would be in Gulfport. He would eat steaks and lobster and sleep on clean sheets. He imagined turning the air conditioning at the hotel down very low.

He lay in the shade and dozed until mid-afternoon. He wished he had the manuscript with him so he could have spent the afternoon translating the next section.

Before leaving he filtered enough water to fill all the water jugs. The water would turn brackish as they neared the Gulf. The salt would clog the filters.

He poled the boat through the narrow channels. He reached the end of the marsh, which gave way to a stand of cypresses. He consulted the map. More marsh was on the other side. So he entered the labyrinth of trees, following a compass bearing.

At dusk he came out of the swamp and into the marsh again. As he poled the boat along a channel, he kept the Mannlicher on the seat at his feet. He was hoping to surprise a marsh deer, small animals which had adapted to life in the marsh. They lived on the hummocks and islands.

For an hour he hunted this way until he poled the boat around a bend in a channel and surprised three marsh deer, all does. He raised the rifle and dropped one in her tracks.

He poled he boat to an island and made camp. He gutted the deer, which he hung from a limb of a live oak.

He roasted a haunch over a fire and stuffed himself with meat. Then he sat close to the fire, using the smoke to keep away the mosquitoes, Gators grunted from the marsh; a night bird called; an owl flew into the light of the fire, passing through the smoke on silent wings.

He coated himself with a fresh layer of mud and went to sleep by the fire, wondering if he would dream of Octavius.

He awoke suddenly to a slapping sound. It was dark. The fire had burnt down to ashes. He grabbed a stick out of the fire and whirled it about his head. The end glowed and then burst into flame. In the light from the stick he saw that an enormous gator, as long as the boat, was after the deer, standing beneath it and lunging toward it with open jaws. Its jaws made the slapping sound again as it went for the deer and missed.

He picked up the rifle, holding it against his shoulder with one hand and the burning stick above his head with the other. The gator turned and looked toward him, its eye shine glowing red in the light from the torch. He expected it to run, but it did not. Instead it regarded him gravely, almost with sagacity. He imagined the bullet striking it in some vulnerable spot and having no effect at all. For an instant he had a picture in his mind of Paul climbing the iron ladder with angry hornets swarming about him.

No, he thought. *It's too damned big. It's time to leave something alone.*

He lowered the rifle. The gator tried again for the deer, this time reaching it. The rope broke with a snap. The gator dragged the carcass off into the water faster than he would have thought possible and disappeared.

He slept no more that night. He sat by the fire with the rifle, listening to the sounds from the swamp: grunts from gators, a mad chorus of frogs, the splash of a fish, and the calls of night birds. Finally the sky lightened, which was soon filled flights of ducks and wading birds. The sun rose red and swollen in the tops of a line of cypresses.

He swam in the water off the island. He imagined the gator lying in the grass full of deer meat. Strangely he felt no fear. Then he located a cooler spot in the water, perhaps the result of some underground spring. He lingered in the spot, treading water. A cottonmouth swam by twenty yards away, a gar flopped to the surface, its scales bright in the sunlight, a heron stalked fish in the shallows. He wondered what Paul would have seen if he had been beside him, Paul who claimed to be able to see the insides of things. He stayed there waiting, but nothing was revealed to him. Exhausted he swam to shore.

After he plastered himself with mud, he took to the boat again. The marsh soon gave way to another cypress swamp. He followed a slough through it all morning. According to the map he was not far from the last highway bridge over the Pearl.

He stopped to fish and caught a nice bass, which he wrapped

in mud and baked over a fire on a hummock for lunch.

As he dozed in the shade of a bay tree, he wished Paul were with him. Paul would have liked the big gator. And he thought of how that if Mason had been there he would have tried to kill it. If Mason had been successful, Henry would have measured it and counted its teeth and examined the contents of its stomach.

He thought of Octavius. He wondered if Octavius had loved Mary, for there was nothing so far in the narrative to make Robert certain that was true. He had wanted to take her to Haiti, make a life with her. But neither one of them had had time for love. Perhaps he had found some woman in Haiti whom he loved. But then why had he come back after he had gone to Haiti and become rich and become a Duke? Perhaps the woman who was mistress of the big white house on the hill above the sea had died.

He wished he could understand why he returned to Mississippi. It seemed to him that Octavius would have gone to Europe. Maybe Italy. Mississippi was in more chaos than Haiti. What civilization there was had been destroyed, transformed. But he would never know. Unless the answer was in the sea chapters or Haiti or even Paris.

Then he found himself thinking of Elaine. He imagined himself telling someone in a bar in Gulfport what had happened to Elaine and how he missed her and how his grief did not seem to have an end. If Mason or Henry had been with him, he would have told them. But Paul would have been the best audience. He would have told it to Paul at night as they sat around the fire, after they had eaten their fill of venison or fish and were drinking whiskey. Paul would have understood.

He looked up at the vacant blue sky. Far off in the direction of the sea he saw a flight of large white birds. He watched them until they disappeared. Then a vulture sailed into view. He supposed it had been there all the time, turning in slow circles just beyond his range of vision. It came closer and he began to wonder if it were Hoffman. But that was not likely since it came from the direction of the sea. Far away across the marsh was a line of cypress. The treetops shimmered in the heat. He would pole the boat through that maze of channels and eventually reach the sea.

Soon the vulture was almost directly overhead. It might think that he was potential food. He took up the field glasses and trained them on the bird. The vulture sprang into view. A piece of red bandana was tied around its left leg. As he watched Hoffman turn his head to look down at him, he wondered if Hoffman thought Paul was still alive and was searching for him.

Hoffman circled lower and lower and finally sailed down to land in the open space before him. The bird walked up close to him with his hopping sort of gait. Then he stood there within arm's length. The bird cocked his head to one side and looked at him. Robert offered Hoffman a piece of the fish, but the bird did not seem interested.

The bird pulled himself up to his full height and stretched out his wings. For a moment Robert thought he was going to take flight but he did not. He folded up his wings and turned his eye on Robert again. Robert felt uncomfortable in his gaze.

"Paul's dead," Robert said.

But he expected that Hoffman knew Paul was dead. After all the bird was an expert on death. Robert looked about and suddenly felt small and helpless amid that glittering flatness of water and mud and grass that lay between him and the sea. He looked at Hoffman who was standing so perfectly still that he might have been a bird carved out of cypress. .

"Once my wife went to Africa," Robert began, knowing as he spoke that he was going to tell it all.

Scott Ely was born in Atlanta, GA, and he moved to Jackson, MS when he was eight. He served in Vietnam (somewhere in the highlands near Pleiku). He graduated with an MFA from the University of Arkansas, Fayetteville. He teaches fiction writing at Winthrop University in South Carolina. His previous book publications include PULPWOOD (Livingston Press); STARLIGHT (Weidenfeld & Nicolson); PITBULL (Weidenfeld & Nicolson, Penguin); OVERGROWN WITH LOVE (University of Arkansas Press); THE ANGEL OF THE GARDEN (University of Missouri Press). His work has been translated in Italy, Germany, Israel, Poland, and Japan. There were also UK editions of the novels published.

Previous (and forthcoming) Magazine Publications:

Playboy; Southern Review; Baton Rouge; LA; Antioch Review; Gettysburg Review; New Letters; Shenandoah; Five Points; 21st: A Journal of Contemporary Photography.